A Jaine Austen Mystery

PAMPERED to DEATH

LAURA LEVINE

KENSINGTON BOOKS
www.kensingtonbooks.com

efore long I was in the middle of ⟨h⟩eavenly ⟨…⟩ing me. George Cloo⟨…⟩ a vat of gu⟨…⟩e. But th⟨…⟩ ju⟨…⟩aⱤG⟨…⟩ his-pering sweet nothings in my ear, he st⟨a⟩rted screaming at the top of his lungs.

Oh, crud. He must've gotten a good look at my thighs.

His screams grew louder and louder, and frankly I was beginning to get a bit ticked off. Okay, so he was a major motion picture star. And I was just a Weight Watchers dropout. But a girl's got feelings, you know.

Then suddenly I realized it wasn't George screaming, but a woman.

It wasn't a dream. Those screams were real!

I sat up with a jolt, and indeed the voice I heard was Shawna's, wailing from Mallory's cubicle next door.

I jumped down off the massage table and, draped in a towel, I hurried out to the corridor.

Shawna was standing in the doorway of Mallory's cubicle, still screaming at full throttle.

And with good reason.

As I peered over Shawna's shoulder, I saw Mallory lying on her massage table, strangled with a hunk of bull kelp . . .

Books by Laura Levine

THIS PEN FOR HIRE

LAST WRITES

KILLER BLONDE

SHOES TO DIE FOR

THE PMS MURDER

DEATH BY PANTYHOSE

CANDY CANE MURDER

KILLING BRIDEZILLA

KILLER CRUISE

DEATH OF A TROPHY WIFE

GINGERBREAD COOKIE MURDER

PAMPERED TO DEATH

DEATH OF A NEIGHBORHOOD WITCH

Published by Kensington Publishing Corporation

For my darling Gracie, in memory of her beloved
"Vegas" Bob Kastner—IOV both forever.

ACKNOWLEDGMENTS

As always, I am enormously grateful to my editor John Scognamiglio for his unwavering faith in Jaine, and to my agent Evan Marshall for his valued guidance and support. Thanks to Hiro Kimura for making Prozac such a fabulous cover girl, and to Lou Malcangi for his eye-catching dust jacket.

Special thanks to Frank Mula, man of a thousand jokes. To Maxine Skolnick, for launching DaddyO's political career. And to Joanne Fluke, who takes time out from writing her own best-selling Hannah Swenson mysteries to grace me with her insights and her brownies—not to mention a blurb to die for.

Thanks to Marshall Field and Amie "Simone" Norden, at the beautiful Burke Williams Spa in Santa Monica, whose seaweed wrap is sheer heaven and not the least bit fatal. To Leslee Matsushige at the Scripps Institute of Oceanography, for supplying me with fun facts about kelp. And to Mike Gargano at the Beverly Hills Country Club, for showing me how a "Fat Vat" works and who is in no way responsible for any errors I may have made in describing it.

To Ky and Jennifer at Bristol Farms in Westwood, two of the world's finest (and friendliest) supermarket checkers. To Mark Baker, who was there from the beginning. And to John Fluke, product placement guru and all-around great guy.

A loving thanks to my friends and family for hanging in with me all these years. And a special shout out to all the readers who've taken the time to write me and/or show up at my book signings. Muchas, muchas gracias!

And finally, to my most loyal fan and sounding board, my husband Mark. I couldn't do it without you.

Chapter 1

Driving with my cat Prozac gives new meaning to the words "hell on wheels." On the day my story begins, she was at her very worst—crouched in her travel carrier on the passenger seat of my car, wailing at the top of her lungs.

Are we there yet?
Are we there yet?
Are we there yet?
Are we there yet?
Are we there yet?
Are we there yet?

And I hadn't even put the key in the ignition. "Can't you please be quiet?" I begged.

She glared up at me from her deluxe sherpa-lined carrier and erupted in a fresh batch of wails.

This screeching would go on for hours, but I could not afford to let Prozac out of her carrier, not unless I was prepared to have her pee on the upholstery and do the cha cha on the gas pedal. I have learned from bitter experience—and near-fatal accidents—never to allow my frisky feline to roam free in a moving vehicle.

I did my best to tune her out as I started the car and focused on my destination. Believe it or not, I, Jaine Austen—a gal whose idea of a spa treatment is a soak in the tub with my good buddy Mr. Bubble—was headed up the California coast to The Haven, a swellegant spa for the rich and pampered.

This fabulous treat was a gift from my next door neighbor, Lance Venable. Mind you, Lance does not normally go around showering me with expensive gifts (or any gifts for that matter), but this was his way of thanking me for getting him off the hook for murder (a fascinating tale, which you can read all about in *Death of a Trophy Wife*, now available in paperback at all the usual places).

Not only did Lance foot the bill for an all-expenses-paid week at The Haven, he'd also forked over extra bucks so Prozac could stay with me.

A gesture I sorely wished he hadn't bothered to make.

Still trying to tune out her piercing wails, I thought back to the day Lance had given me my gift.

We were sitting on his living room sofa, sipping Diet Cokes and snacking on corn chips.

"I suppose you're wondering why I asked you to stop by," he said.

"You got something stuck in your garbage disposal, and you want me to put my hand down to find it?"

One of his favorite requests.

"No, silly. I bought you a present!"

He reached behind a sofa cushion and took out a beautifully wrapped gift box. "Just a little something for saving my life."

"You shouldn't have, Lance," I demurred. Of course I didn't mean it. If it hadn't been for me, he'd be sitting in jail in a most unflattering orange jumpsuit.

Eagerly I clawed at the box's silk ribbons, hoping for a pair of dangly earrings or maybe a bottle of fancy perfume. Ripping it open, I peeked inside.

"Oh." My smile froze. "A piece of paper. How nice."

"Read it," he said. "It's a gift certificate to The Haven!"

"The Haven? Wow, that's fabulous, Lance. Just terrific."

"You have no idea what The Haven is, do you?"

"No," I confessed.

"It's only one of the most exclusive spas in the country. You're going to spend an entire week lolling in the lap of luxury, having each and every one of your clogged pores deep-cleaned."

I wasn't so sure about the pore cleaning thing, but a week of lolling sounded darn good to me.

"Oh, Lance! How can I ever thank you?"

"You can start by passing me the chips."

I passed him the bowl of of reduced-sodium,

low-fat cardboard posing as corn chips. Lance insists on eating all sorts of ghastly low-cal food, an enthusiasm I do not share. When it comes to calories, my motto has always been The More, the Merrier.

Eventually we polished off our Diet Cokes and I bid him a fond farewell.

"Next time I see you," I promised, "I'll have the cleanest pores in all of Los Angeles."

And now, just days later, I was on my way to The Haven.

True, Prozac continued to whine nonstop for the next two hundred and thirty-seven miles. But I didn't care. I was about to spend a week luxuriating in manis, massages, and poolside margaritas.

Or so I thought.

Little did I know that also on the schedule was a little thing called murder.

Chapter 2

At first glance, The Haven was indeed quite haven-ly. A sprawling Spanish style hacienda with red tile roof and magnificent arched windows, it stood beneath a canopy of pines, high in the hills of a rustic town on the central coast of California.

It was smaller than I'd expected, more like a private residence than a resort hotel.

But that made it all the more charming.

I pulled my Corolla into a gravel parking lot at the side of the house, and for the first time in hours, Prozac finally stopped wailing.

"We're here, honeybunny!"

She glared up at me from her carrier.

I want a divorce.

With no parking attendant in sight, I grabbed Prozac's carrier and my suitcase and made my way to the front door, stepping into a soaring two-story reception area. An elaborate wrought iron staircase wended its way to the second floor.

Nestled in a nook beside the staircase was the spa's receptionist, a middle-aged woman who wore her graying blond hair in a thick braid down her back.

She was on the phone as I walked in, but mouthed that she'd be right with me.

"Our spa package starts at $400 a day," she was saying to her caller, "depending on your accommodations."

Four hundred bucks day? I almost fainted dead on the spot.

Apparently so had the caller.

"Yes, I know it's a little high, but it's well worth it . . . No, I'm afraid we don't offer AARP discounts."

While the receptionist yakked about shiatsu massages and aromatherapy, I took a look around. To my left was a dining room, set with crisp white linens, and to my right a spacious lounge with an exposed wood-beam ceiling and a fireplace big enough to park my Corolla.

"Well, give us a ring when you're ready to make a reservation," the receptionist said as she wrapped up her call, clearly unhappy to have let a customer slip through her fingers. Probably worked on commission.

Then she turned to me with a bright smile, the kind they teach you in Bed and Breakfast school.

"Welcome to The Haven!" When she got up to shake my hand, I saw she was nearly six feet tall, with the shoulders of a Valkyrie, a middle-aged poster girl for *Triumph of the Will.*

"I'm Olga Truitt, owner and proprietor."

How odd that the owner was manning the reception desk. At a ritzy joint like this, I'd expect her to have minions aplenty to answer the phone.

"You must be Jaine. I recognized you from your *Cuckoo for Cocoa Puffs* T-shirt. The fellow who made your reservations told me about your appalling taste in clothes."

Okay, so she used the word *eccentric* instead of *appalling,* but I knew darn well what Lance must have told her. For some insane reason, Lance insists moths come to my closet to commit suicide.

"This must be your kitty," she said, kneeling down to get a better look at Prozac. "Let's get her out of that cage."

"I wouldn't if I were you," I warned as Olga reached for the latch on the carrier. "I'm afraid she's a little cranky right now."

Which was, of course, the understatement of the millennium. At that moment Prozac was a cross between Godzilla and a Real Housewife of New Jersey.

"Don't be silly," Olga said, flipping open the latch.

I cringed in dismay as she reached inside, imagining her chiseled cheekbones crisscrossed with bloody scratches.

But Prozac, as she often is with strangers, was a perfect angel. She leaped into Olga's arms like her long-lost daughter and stared up at her lovingly.

Thank heavens you've rescued me. You can't imagine how this dreadful woman mistreats me.

"Somebody here could stand to lose a few pounds," said Olga, bouncing her in her arms.

You're telling me. You should see how she eats between meals. I'm surprised she can still fit into her elastic waist jeans.

"Let me show you to your room." Olga lifted my heavy suitcase as if it were a feather duster.

With Prozac nestled in one arm and my suitcase in the other, she led the way down a hallway to a series of bedrooms at the rear of the house.

Once more I was puzzled. Since when do owners of fancy-dancy spas have to tote their guests' suitcases? Don't they have bellhops for stuff like that? And as we walked down the corridor, I couldn't help but notice that the walls could have used a touch of fresh paint.

"We pride ourselves on a very intimate atmosphere here at The Haven," Olga said, "catering to just a handful of guests."

She stopped at one of the carved wooden doors along the hallway and opened it with an old fashioned key.

"Here we are," she said, ushering me inside.

Aside from a slightly threadbare bedspread, it was a beautiful high-ceilinged room with a four-poster bed and antique armoire. A bowl of fresh-cut flowers graced a dresser, and gorgeous French doors led out to a screened-in patio.

"So what do you think of your home away from home?" Olga asked Prozac, plopping her down on the floor.

Prozac took an exploratory sniff or two, then looked up at the bed inquisitively.

What? No chocolates on the pillow?

Okay, I have no idea if that's what Prozac was thinking, but I sure was. I happen to like the whole chocolate-on-the-pillow thing when I travel. It's so much nicer than those silly free shower caps they give you that never even begin to cover your hair.

"Her litter box is out on the patio," Olga informed me, "and her food and water bowls are in the bathroom. Why don't you get settled, and then I'll take you on a tour of the facilities. After that, it's cocktail hour!"

She marched off with a cheery wave, her Valkyrie braid bouncing in her wake.

After she left, I checked out the bathroom, impressed with its mosaic tiles and claw footed bathtub. There, as promised, next to a pedestal sink, were a pair of earthenware bowls for Prozac.

Lance had assured me The Haven would provide the best in chow for both me and my hungry roommate.

And by now I was starving. I'd wanted to stop off for a burger on the drive up, but couldn't possibly prolong the agony of Prozac's wails.

I thought longingly of the gourmet food sure to come. I couldn't wait to dig into the hors d'oeuvres at cocktail hour. What's more, The Haven was a mere grape's throw from the central California wineries, so I eagerly awaited a glass of nerve-soothing chardonnay to accompany my snacks.

After hanging my clothes in a closet that smelled of lavender and mothballs, I left Prozac sunning herself on the screened-in patio and set off for a tour of the facilities, counting the milliseconds till cocktail hour.

"This is my pride and joy!"

Olga and I were standing in the middle of a large vegetable garden at the back of the house.

"Aren't they beautiful?" she asked, gazing lovingly at the beds of lettuce, carrots, zucchini, tomatoes, and herbs at her feet.

Not nearly as beautiful, in my humble op, as a sausage pizza dripping with cheese, but I nodded in agreement, faking a nature-loving smile.

"All the produce on our menu comes from right here in this garden." She kneeled down to fondle a tomato. "It's all organic of course. Nothing toxic ever goes near my little angels."

She squeezed a leaf, and held it under my nose. A pungent aroma assaulted my nostrils.

"Cilantro. Isn't it heavenly?"

Frankly, I'd smelled sweat socks with a nicer bouquet. But I forced another nature-loving grin.

Shooting one last tender glance at her "angels," she resumed our tour, leading me out of the garden to the pool area at the rear of the house.

The pool was a vintage beauty, a turquoise gem bordered with vibrant Mexican tiles. Nearby, beneath the shade of a towering pine, a jacuzzi sent plumes of steam into the cool afternoon air.

Olga eyed a faded blonde who sat on a chaise reading a copy of *People* magazine, and said to me, "So far you and Ms. Kane are the only guests who've checked in. Let me introduce you.

"Hello, Cathy," she called out, leading me over to my spa-mate, who looked up from her *People* with pale blue eyes. From the extra padding she sported around her hip/thigh zone, I figured she was a fellow member of the Ben & Jerry Fan Club.

"I'd like you to meet our new arrival, Jaine Austen. This is Jaine's first trip to The Haven."

Cathy's eyes lit up.

"Really? Me, too! I've been dreaming about coming here for years, and at last I finally made it!" She gazed in awe at her bucolic surroundings. "You're going to just love everything, Jaine! Olga took me on the tour earlier. It's all so fabulous!"

At four hundred bucks a day, I thought, it darn well better be.

"See you later for cocktails, Cathy," Olga said. "Time to finish showing Jaine around."

And she was just about to lead me away, when a breathy voice trilled out behind us, "Yoo hoo! Olga, honey!"

We turned to see a stunning tawny-haired woman sweeping down the path with what looked like a fur muffler in her arms.

"Omigosh!" Cathy gasped, fanning herself with

her *People*. "Isn't that Mallory Francis, the movie star?"

Olga's face clouded over.

"Well, she's not exactly a star," she muttered. "The woman hasn't been in a hit film in years."

True, but thanks to a series of high profile divorces and a centerfold in *Playboy*, Mallory Francis had been constant tabloid fodder and the star of many a Lifetime movie, not to mention her own highly-rated reality show, *Mad About Mallory*.

Like Cathy, I'd recognized her right away.

Now she came gliding over, a vision in tight white jeans and halter top, her creamy skin spray tanned to perfection.

Perched in the crook of her arms was not a muffler, after all, but a wiry Pekinese whose huge brown eyes glittered with malice.

"Olga, honey," Mallory cried. "So wonderful to see you! Armani," she prompted her pooch, "give Olga-Wolga a gweat big kiss."

The peke let out an ominous growl, baring a set of rather terrifying little fangs.

"Bad doggie," Mallory chided, her mouth puckered in mock disapproval.

Stifling what I was certain was a growl of her own, Olga managed a stiff smile. "Welcome back to The Haven, Mallory."

"So fabulous to be here." Mallory planted an air kiss somewhere in the general vicinity of Olga's cheek. "Don't worry about showing me to my suite. I can see you have your hands full with these two nobodies."

Okay, so she didn't really call us nobodies, but I could tell that's what she was thinking by the dismissive glance she'd shot in our direction.

"I'll have someone on your staff let me in," she said to Olga. "But I just couldn't check in without saying hello!"

She paused to look around.

"The place hasn't changed a bit. That's what I love about The Haven. Other spas are constantly making improvements, but The Haven stays the same year after year." She paused to finger a frayed piece of mesh on one of the pool chairs. "That's what makes it so charming."

Correct me if I'm wrong, but that was a bit of a dig, *n'est-ce pas?*

"I'm so happy you approve," Olga replied, icicles dripping from her voice.

I'd sensed friendlier vibes at a shark tank.

"Well, I'm off to my suite," Mallory chirped. "Send up an order of fresh mangoes, will you, hon? I've got the munchies."

And away she sailed, high heels clacking on the flagstones.

Cathy stared after her, slack-jawed.

"Omigosh!" she gasped. "I can't believe I get to spend a whole week with Mallory Francis!"

"Me, neither," Olga said with a weary sigh. "Me, neither."

The next stop on our itinerary was the Spa Therapy Center.

A squat box of a building, clearly built decades after the main house, it held a rabbit warren of massage rooms, separated down the middle by a narrow corridor. At one end of the corridor sat a large urn, which was where, according to Olga, The Haven's special muscle-relaxing tea—imported all the way from Tibet—was served daily.

Olga showed me one of the massage rooms, a no-frills affair featuring a massage table, supply cabinet, and—over in the corner of the room—a large metal vat. At first I thought it might be some kind of high-tech hamper.

But then Olga said, "That's where we keep the seaweed for our detoxifying seaweed wraps."

"Seaweed wraps?"

The only wraps I knew involved lunch meat and pita bread.

"They suck up all the nasty toxins from your body. Most ordinary spas use a paste for their seaweed wraps. But here at The Haven we add real seaweed for extra detoxification."

With that, she lifted the lid and hauled out an enormous piece of bull kelp, the kind you see strung along the shoreline after a storm, usually buzzing with sand flies.

"It's been thoroughly sterilized," Olga assured me, "and preserved in a protein-enriched brine. You can't imagine how wonderful it feels to be wrapped up with one of these babies for forty-five minutes."

Now I'm as fond of a dip in the ocean as the next guy (so long as the next guy isn't the captain of the *Titanic*), but the last thing I wanted was to get up close and personal with a piece of algae.

But I nodded as if I actually believed her.

"Okay," she said, returning the kelp to its brine, "now it's time for a tour of the kitchen."

At last, she was talking my language.

Chapter 3

The Haven's gourmet chef turned out to be a gawky teenager named Kevin. He was busy chopping vegetables when Olga and I showed up in the kitchen, a huge outdated affair whose fixtures looked like they'd been installed sometime in the Coolidge administration.

"I'm between chefs right now," Olga explained, "and Kevin has been helping me out after school. He's really marvelously talented."

"With the experience I gain here," he told me solemnly from beneath a mop of unruly bangs, "I hope someday to get a job at Applebee's."

So much for gourmet dining.

But I didn't mind. At home, my idea of fine dining is adding Dijon mustard to my Quarter Pounder, so I was certainly up for some simple fare. A T-bone smothered in A1 Steak Sauce would suit me just fine.

"Mallory Francis and her people showed up a little while ago," Kevin said.

"I know," Olga sighed.

"I took them to their rooms." He hacked away at some cilantro. "Mallory stiffed me on the tip."

"What a surprise," Olga muttered.

"And she wants mangoes for dessert tonight. She said to be sure they're fresh."

"I'll bet she did," Olga said, a tiny vein beginning to throb in her forehead.

She reached for a big bottle of pills on the large pine island that dominated the kitchen.

"Vitamins," she said, popping two of them in her mouth. "Have to keep up my energy."

Meanwhile, I was busy sniffing the room for any signs of dinner in the oven. But all I could smell was that damn cilantro. Oh, well. Maybe there were steaks marinating in the fridge. Or chicken breasts smothered in barbeque sauce. Or perhaps a nice cheesy lasagna, just waiting to be popped in the oven—

My food fantasies were interrupted when Olga thrust a piece of paper in my hand.

"Here's a copy of tonight's menu."

Now my heart didn't actually stop when I read that menu, but it came pretty darn close. *Quel* nightmare. A depressing 300-calorie affair, it featured *fresh garden salad, vegetable medley,* and two words that sent my taste buds running for cover—*steamed fish.*

What can I say? Unless it's lobster, dripping with butter, I am not a fish fan. And *steamed* fish? That meant no outside crispy stuff. Just inside fishy stuff.

Yuck.

"Um, Olga," I said, when I finally managed to regain my powers of speech, "I think there's been a bit of a mistake here."

"What's wrong? Did I misspell *medley* again?"

"No, no. I'm here for the regular menu. The one with the steaks and pasta."

"Steaks and pasta?" Olga laughed gaily. "There are no steaks and pasta, Jaine. Didn't you know? The Haven is a strict diet retreat. All our guests get 900 low-carb calories a day."

I most certainly did *not* know this joint was a diet place. *Au contraire*, Lance had been raving up his wazoo about what divine food they had. If I'd had any idea that I'd be giving up edible food for the next week, I would never have agreed to come.

I mean, why on earth would I want to hang out at a place that did not believe in the dessert fairy?

"I'm sorry," I said, "but you're just going to have to issue my friend a refund. I'm checking out."

"No can do," Olga replied, her Valkyrie arms clamped firmly across her chest. "We don't issue refunds here at The Haven."

Oh, crud. This place must have cost Lance a small fortune. I couldn't let all that money go to waste. The least I could do was stick it out for a few days.

And so, in a moment to be filed in my Worst Decisions Ever department, I said:

"Okay, I'll give it a try."

* * *

Back at my room, I found Prozac stretched out on the patio flagstones, soaking up the sun.

"Horrible news, Pro," I moaned, slumping down on the chaise next to her. "The Haven is a 900-calorie-a-day diet spa! How on earth am I going to live on nine hundred itsy bitsy calories a day?"

She looked up at me in that comforting way of hers, as if to say:

You could start by giving me a belly rub.

"Nine hundred calories! Most of them from smelly green stuff."

And while you're at it, could you scratch me behind my ears?

"That's a whole week without the three basic food groups: chocolate, pizza, and Chunky Monkey."

I don't feel you scratching.

"My God, Pro. Don't you see what this means? I'm in diet hell."

She peered at me through slitted eyes.

Aw, quit your beefing. If you ask me, this place is heaven. Why can't we have a patio like this at home?

At which point, my pity party was interrupted by a knock on my door. Wearily, I dredged myself out of the chaise and went to get it.

I opened the door to find Olga standing there, with what looked like a fishing rod in one hand and an oversized hamster wheel in the other.

"Your cat's too fat," she announced without preamble.

Out on the patio, Prozac looked up in surprise.

Surely she can't mean moi *?*

"She needs to work out. So I brought her some exercise equipment.

"This," Olga said, dropping the oversized hamster wheel on the carpet, "is a kitty treadmill. And this"—she waved the fishing rod, which I now saw had some fake feathers hanging from it—"is a Whirly Bird."

If you squinted really hard and were standing in the next county, the feathers on the fishing rod vaguely resembled a bird.

"Yes," she said, "we'll whittle those ugly pounds off the two of you in no time."

Someone certainly flunked out of Tact 101.

Olga marched out to the patio and, scooping Prozac into her arms, brought her back inside.

Prozac bristled with annoyance.

Hey wait a minute. I was in the middle of a very important nap!

Then she wriggled free from Olga's grasp and jumped to the floor, heading back out to the patio.

But Olga quickly shut the patio door, closing off her escape route, and began waving the Whirly Bird.

"Watch," she said. "She'll think it's a bird and go chasing after it."

As if.

Prozac took one look at that thing in action and practically rolled her eyes in disbelief.

Lady, you gotta be kidding. If that's a bird, I'm an Airedale.

With that, she plopped down on the carpet and began an intense perusal of her genitals.

"That's funny," Olga mused. "Most cats go crazy over the Whirly Bird."

"Prozac's not like most cats."

"So I see. A little slow, is she?"

Honestly, sometimes I swear Prozac understands English. She actually tore herself away from her genitals long enough to give Olga a most unfriendly hiss.

I can't say I blamed her.

"Prozac is not the least bit slow," I said, leaping to my pampered princess's defense. "She happens to be smarter than many people I know."

Several of whom, I might add, are currently serving in Congress.

"Well, let's try the kitty treadmill," Olga chirped, her enthusiasm undampened.

Snatching Prozac from her genital exam, she deposited her on the treadmill.

It was a lot like the exercise wheels you see in hamster cages, only instead of wire, the track was solid wood.

"Now we'll just tempt her with a dietetic kitty treat." Olga pulled out a small can of something called Cardio Cat Nips and placed a few on the treadmill. "Made with no artificial colors, no artificial flavors, no artificial preservatives."

"Actually," I pointed out, "those happen to be three of her favorite things."

Prozac, who has been known to nosh on unwashed gym socks, sniffed at the Cardio Nips in disgust, and then curled up on the treadmill to resume her perusal of her privates.

"She'll get the hang of it," Olga said. "You've just got to be firm with her." And then, her voice dripping with disapproval, she added, "She didn't get this fat without an enabler."

Of all the nerve. By now, I felt like hissing at her myself.

"I almost forgot!" Olga said. "Her cat food."

She trotted out to the hallway and carted in a basket of canned cat food.

"It's a low cal, low fat, vitamin-enriched, hairball control formula with special enzymes to promote healthy digestion."

Prozac eyed it warily as Olga popped the pull tab and held it under her nose.

This was the last straw.

One sniff and Prozac bolted across the room to hide under the bed.

Never had I seen her so freaked. This is a cat who never hides under the bed. Not even during an earthquake.

"A lot of cats don't like it at first," Olga said. "But she'll get used to it in no time. Especially," she sneered, "when there's nothing else to eat."

Then, smiling what I considered a most sadistic smile, she headed for the door.

Good heavens. The woman was a regular Diet Nazi.

The minute she was gone, Prozac poked her head out from under the dust ruffle, and stared up at me with frantic green eyes.

We gotta break outta this dump!

Chapter 4

I headed over to the lounge for cocktail hour, praying that actual cocktails would be served. If not cocktails, a simple glass of wine. Surely Olga could spare a hundred or so calories on some chardonnay.

Not bloody likely.

The cocktail Olga thrust into my hand when I showed up was a puke green concoction called a celery fizz. (Half celery juice, half club soda, and a sprig of arugula—for those of you masochistic enough to try it.)

"Bottoms up," Olga commanded.

Good heavens. The woman actually expected me to drink it.

I took a tentative sip, prompting my taste buds to recoil in horror.

I do not exaggerate when I say the stuff tasted like carbonated lawn clippings. (Not that I've ever tasted lawn clippings, but they can't possibly be worse than that ghastly celery fizz.)

I thought about tossing it into a nearby potted palm when Olga wasn't looking, but I was afraid it might kill the palm.

"Let me introduce you to everyone," Olga said as she ushered me into the lounge, where overstuffed armchairs and sofas shrouded in shabby chic slipcovers were scattered about like huge chintz mushrooms. Cathy, the pale blonde I'd met at the pool, was sitting in one of the chairs near the fireplace watching a rather anemic fire as it sputtered to stay alive.

"Hi, Jaine!" she said, catching sight of me.

I waved hello as Olga led me past her to meet two more fellow inmates who were sitting together on a loveseat.

"Jaine, meet Harvy, Mallory Francis's personal hair stylist."

A reed thin guy clad in fashionably wrinkled linen beamed me a dazzling smile.

"Love your hair, sweetheart," he said, eyeing my mop of unruly curls. "It's so Nouveau Harpo Marx."

I suspected that was a bit of a slam, but I decided to take the high road and smiled anyway.

"And this,"—Olga nodded at the woman sitting next to Harvy, a dour gal with wire-rimmed glasses and what I would soon discover was a permanent scowl—"is Kendra, Mallory's personal assistant."

Kendra grunted a curt hello, her lips puckered in a sour expression. But that, of course, might have been due to the celery fizz.

"Come sit by me, Jaine," Cathy beckoned from across the room, patting the armchair next to her.

Sensing Kendra was not enamored of my company, I took Cathy up on her offer, and trotted over to join her.

"We're closer to the snacks over here," Cathy whispered as I sat down next to her.

The snacks to which she referred, set out on a coffee table in front of us, were a depressing collection of carrot and celery sticks, garnished with some carelessly washed radishes.

"This is going to be a lot harder than I thought," Cathy said, picking up a celery stick with a sigh. "But it's all going to be worth it in the end. I intend to drop at least five pounds while I'm here. Gosh, I still can't believe I'm actually staying at The Haven."

"It's unbelievable, all right," I muttered.

"I thought I'd die when I realized Mallory Francis was here, too. I see her all the time at work."

"You work for her, too?" I blinked, puzzled.

"Oh, I don't see her in person. I see her picture in the tabloids. I'm a supermarket checker—which isn't easy, I can tell you. Standing next to those candy bar racks all day, it's no wonder I've put on a few pounds over the years. Sometimes I think of chucking it all and going into cosmetology, but I can't risk losing my pension. Oh, well. Only twelve more years till retirement, but who's counting. Haha. So what kind of work do you do, Jaine?"

It took me a while to realize she'd actually

taken time out from her bio to ask me a question.

"Me? I'm a writer."

"A writer? Omigosh! First a TV movie star. And now, a writer! What books have you written?"

I was about to tell her I was not a novelist but a freelance copywriter and as such the only book I'd ever written was a stirring opus for Toiletmasters Plumbers called *You and Your Septic Tank.* But I never did get a chance to break the disappointing news, because just then Mallory Francis made her grand entrance.

And I do mean grand.

"Sorry I'm late, everybody," she crooned from the doorway.

All eyes were riveted on her as she came sailing into the room on legs that wouldn't quit, her tawny mane of sun-streaked hair billowing out behind her.

My God, the woman was a walking Victoria's Secret commercial.

Perched in the crook of her arm was her petulant Peke.

"Say hello to everyone, Armani." Mallory prompted.

Armani gave an angry yip, eyeing us with the imperious air of a dog who'd been a third world despot in a former life.

Both Mallory and the Peke wore matching turquoise T-shirts, emblazoned with rhinestone lettering that said *Danger. High Maintenance.*

"Olga, honey!" Mallory said, catching sight of our genial hostess.

Once again, I sensed tension in the air.

"You know I hate to complain—"

Behind her back I could see Kendra rolling her eyes.

"—but my towels are just the weensiest bit threadbare. I need some new ones ASAP. You know the kind I like."

"Yes," Olga said, a nasty glint in her eye, "so fluffy you can hardly close your suitcase."

"Ha ha ha!" Mallory didn't even try to make it sound like a laugh. "That's what I love about you, Olga, you're so very amusing."

Then she narrowed her eyes and added, "I see you still haven't called that plastic surgeon I told you about. You really ought to, hon. The man's a positive miracle worker. Not that I've ever been to him myself."

Oh, please. She'd been nipped and tucked more times than a thrift shop prom dress.

"Go see Dr. Frankel, honey," Mallory urged, "and those icky crows' feet of yours will be gone in no time."

Olga looked like she wanted to bop her over the head with a celery fizz. Instead she just handed her one.

"Dear God, no!" Mallory moaned. "Not another celery fizz! Hasn't anyone ever told you these things are revolting?"

"You do, Mallory dear. Every year."

"Touchy!" Mallory replied brightly.

I couldn't tell if she was commenting on Olga's emotional state or just mangling the word *touché*.

"Let me introduce you to our newcomers,"

Olga said, leading Mallory over to where Cathy and I were seated. "I never got a chance to do it earlier today."

"I can't get over how gorgeous she is," Cathy whispered as Mallory approached.

And indeed, try as I might, I could not spot a single pore on the woman's flawless face.

Olga proceeded to make introductions, Mallory smiling blandly as our names were announced.

All the while, Armani eyed us, fangs bared, as if we were the hors d'oeuvres.

"I'm so thrilled to meet you, Ms. Francis," Cathy gushed.

"I'm sure you are, sweetie."

"Would you mind awfully autographing my cocktail napkin?"

Cathy thrust the napkin in Mallory's hand before she could object.

"And could you personalize it? To Cathy with a *C*. And Kane with a *K*. It's a good thing my parents didn't name me Candy, huh? Otherwise I'd be Candy Kane! Or Sugar. Then I'd be Sugar Kane. Or Citizen. Then I'd be Citizen Ka—"

"Kendra," Mallory called out, clearly bored with Cathy's name game, "get me a pen."

After her assistant had delivered the requested pen, Mallory scribbled her autograph on the cocktail napkin and handed it to Cathy. (For those of you who care about these kinds of things, she dotted the *i* in Francis with a happy face. And she spelled Kane with a *C*.)

"I'll treasure it forever, Ms. Francis!" Cathy assured her.

"You do that," Mallory said, then drifted over to the loveseat where Harvy and Kendra were seated.

"You don't mind moving, do you, hon?" she asked Kendra. "I want to sit next to Harvy."

Anyone could see this was not a question, but an order.

Her brows knitted in a scowl, Kendra got up and moved to a nearby chair. Mallory took her assistant's place, scooching next to Harvy and giving him an air kiss.

In her arms, Armani growled like a jealous lover.

"Olga, sweetheart," Mallory called out, "would you mind getting Armani a doggie treat? He gets cranky when his blood sugar's too low."

Swallowing her annoyance, Olga pried herself up from the armchair she'd sunk into.

"No problem," she lied, and trotted off down the hallway.

The minute she was gone, Mallory whipped out two miniature vodka bottles from a fanny pack she wore around her tiny waist.

"I'm such a bad girl," she winked at Harvy.

"Thank God for that," Harvy winked back.

Awash in giggles, they twisted open the caps on their vodka bottles and sneaked the booze into their celery fizzes.

Nearby, Kendra sat fuming, clearly ticked off at being excluded from all the fun.

Meanwhile, Cathy was in seventh heaven over her autographed cocktail napkin, yammering about how the minute she got home it was going in her scrapbook, right next to her ticket stub from *Wicked* and her 3-D glasses from *Avatar*.

I was sitting there, trying to tune out her chatter and wishing I had a wee bit of vodka in my celery fizz, when Olga returned, arm in arm with a rugged Marlboro Man lookalike—a muscle-bound dude with chiseled cheekbones and slicked-back hair shiny with gel.

"You all know Clint Masters, don't you?" Olga said.

"Clint Masters?" Cathy cried. "The movie star?"

"Yes, Cathy," Olga said, shooting Mallory a sly smile. "The *A-list* movie star."

And indeed this guy was an A-lister. True, his macho action movies were usually panned by the critics, but were immensely popular with the nineteen-year-old boys who determine what makes a blockbuster.

"Sorry I'm late, everybody," Clint said, flashing us a chemically whitened smile. "Just flew up from L.A., and my limo driver was late picking me up at the airport."

If Olga expected Mallory to be pissed at having to share the spotlight with another celeb, she was sadly mistaken.

"Clint, honey!" Mallory waved him over to the loveseat. "What a wonderful surprise! Olga didn't tell me you'd be staying here."

"She didn't?"

"No, she did not. Naughty Olga!" Mallory wagged a playful finger at her not-so-genial host.

"It's been forever since we've seen each other," Clint said, braving Armani's growl to peck Mallory on the cheek.

"Not since *Revenge of the Lust Busters*. What a fun shoot that was!"

I vaguely remembered a movie they'd made together about cops breaking up an international prostitution ring.

"Scoot, Harvy," she said, shooing away her hairdresser, "so Clint can sit next to me."

Harvy didn't seem to mind having just been demoted. Summoning an ingratiating smile from what I was certain was a vast repertoire, he told Clint how great his hair looked and grabbed a seat near Kendra.

"Olga, darling," Mallory tsked. "I'm still waiting for those doggie treats."

Once again, she wagged an acrylic nail in Olga's direction.

Olga glared at that wagging finger, and as she stormed out of the room, I caught her wagging a most impolite finger of her own.

Chapter 5

I'll spare you the details of the ghastly 300 calories posing as dinner except to say that by the
end of the meal, I would've sold my soul for a
Ding Dong.

A caste system was in effect at The Haven that
night. Mallory and Armani were seated at what
was clearly the "A" table, along with Clint Masters and Harvy the hairdresser.

I was interested to note that Armani (who
came to dinner sporting a sequinned bow tie)
had been somehow exempt from the diet regime,
his doggie bowl filled to the brim with succulent
steak tidbits. It was all I could do to refrain myself from bending down and grabbing a handful.

But, alas, that was not even remotely possible,
as I was seated far from the pampered pooch at
the designated "B" table, along with fellow out-
casts Cathy and Kendra.

Cathy, oblivious to her untouchable status,

was beside herself with joy at the thought of being under the same roof as not one—but *two*—Hollywood celebs.

"Just wait'll I tell the gang at the Piggly Wiggly!"

Kendra, furious at having been banned to Siberia, shot resentful glares at the "A" table, where Harvy was hard at work sucking up to Mallory, going on and on about how fab she looked in the white silk jumpsuit she'd worn to dinner.

"Do you know how many women would kill for a waist like yours?" he gushed.

There were three of us right here at the "B" table at the top of the list.

"Isn't that right, Clint?" Harvy asked his rugged dinner companion. "Doesn't Mallory look fab?"

Clint agreed that Mallory did indeed look fab. But as he sat poking at some puny shards of cilantro, I couldn't help wondering what a studly action hero like Clint Masters was doing at a diet spa. Why the heck wasn't he at some macho hunting lodge, gunning down endangered species?

"So, Mallory," I heard him ask. "What have you been up to?"

Thrilled to be in the spotlight, Mallory proceeded to fill him in on the minutiae of her life—sparing no details—everything from her "simply amazing" new pilates instructor (on call 24 hours a day) to the memoir she'd just signed a deal to write.

At the mention of the memoir, Clint's mega-watt smile seemed to stiffen.

"I read about that in the trades," he said. "Sounds very interesting."

"Oh, it will be," Mallory assured him, with all the confidence of a woman who'd never written two consecutive paragraphs in her life.

"It's going to be just fabulous!" Harvy piped up, in full tilt cheerleader mode.

"It would be," Mallory said, "if only I could find a decent writer to collaborate with."

And by collaborate we all knew she meant someone to write every darn syllable.

"The woman my publisher wants me to work with is totally unsuitable. Would you believe she actually showed up for our first meeting in Birkenstocks!"

"Incredible!" Harvy commiserated, rolling his eyes.

At her feet, Armani took time out from his steak tidbits to yap in disapproval.

"I can't possibly work with a woman who wears Birkenstocks."

"Of course you can't!" cooed Harvy.

"So I'm absolutely desperate for a writer."

Up until this point, Cathy had been enter-taining the "B" table with a detailed summary of her own life as a supermarket checker, and her determination to lose five pounds and connect with Mr. Right (in her case, Earl in the Deli Sec-tion).

But now she took time out from her bio to pipe up:

"You're looking for a writer? Why, Jaine's a writer!"

Oh, for heavens sake. I write toilet bowl brochures, not best-selling memoirs.

But I couldn't really blame Cathy for speaking up. I never did get to fill her in on the specifics of my resumé.

Mallory, who'd been sitting with her back to us, deigned to turn around.

"Which one of you is Jaine?" she asked.

Guess we hadn't made much of an impression at our earlier introductions.

I raised a feeble hand.

She gave me the once over with her cat-like green eyes.

"So you're a writer, huh? You don't wear Birkenstocks, do you?"

"Nope," I said, glad she couldn't see the elastic waist on my L.L.Bean Comfort Fit pants.

"Well," she challenged, "what have you written?"

Now I happen to be quite proud of my magnum opus, *You and Your Septic Tank*. After all, it did win the Golden Plunger Award from the L.A. Plumbers Association. But somehow I sensed it might fail to impress Mallory.

"Go on," Cathy urged. "Tell her."

"*You and Your Septic Tank*," I gulped.

Mallory burst out laughing.

"No, really, hon," she said, when she'd stopped giggling. "What did you write?"

"*You and Your Septic Tank*," I repeated, with as much dignity as I could muster under the circumstances.

"Oh, please," she said, eyeing me as if I'd just emptied a septic tank into her Evian water. "I need a *real* writer."

Normally at humiliating moments like these, I seek solace from my good buddies Ben & Jerry. But as that was out of the question, I just sat there staring at the graying blob of fish on my plate, wishing I could throttle both Mallory and Cathy. Who, incidentally, picked up where they'd left off on their yakathons, each dominating the conversations at their respective tables.

In between anecdotes, Mallory took great pleasure in driving Olga nuts, sending back her fish (undercooked), her string beans (overcooked) and demanding lime slices—not lemon—for her Evian water.

Not only The Haven's owner and receptionist, Olga was apparently its sole waitress, bustling back and forth from the kitchen, trying in vain to satisfy her demanding diva.

And so the meal slogged on, calorie after depressing calorie. I was sitting there in the middle of a most diverting fantasy starring me, George Clooney, and a hot fudge sundae, when Mallory tinkled her glass with a fork.

"Attention, everybody!" she said, standing up to face us all. "I've got an announcement to make."

Armani yapped excitedly, perhaps eager to hear the news, or perhaps hoping for some more steak. He'd daintily polished off his entire bowl, which I must confess, was a bit of a disappointment. I'd been planning to nab a chunk or two after everyone had left the dining room.

(Oh, don't go shaking your head like that. I was starving. And a little dog spit never hurt anybody.)

"After five years as my personal hair stylist," Mallory was saying, "Harvy is embarking on an exciting new phase of his career and opening his own hair salon! Harvé of Beverly Hills! Isn't that just wonderful?"

Harvy beamed at the tepid round of applause that greeted this news.

"And as a token of appreciation for all the years we've been together—not to mention the best highlights in the biz—I'm pleased to announce that I am financing the whole venture!"

Wow. It looked like Harvy's fanny kissing had paid off big time.

Mallory whipped out a folded check from the depths of her cleavage and presented it to him with all the fanfare of King Arthur dubbing a new knight.

Now it was Harvy's turn to lead the applause, which he did with great fervor.

Everyone joined in, except Kendra who sat scowling at Mallory, arms clamped firmly across her chest.

And Armani, who'd decided to take a nap.

At which point, Olga came sailing out from the kitchen with dessert—which turned out to be three pathetic slices of mango per person.

Mallory sniffed at hers suspiciously.

"You sure the mango's fresh?"

"It's fresh!" Olga snapped, stomping back to the kitchen and cutting off any further discussion.

Three mango slices later, my first dinner in hell ground to a merciful halt.

Only five more to go.

I trudged back to my room, opting out of the after-dinner entertainment—an action-packed educational film called *Sugar: The Killer in your Cupboard.*

No sooner had I opened the door than Prozac hurled herself at me, practically frisking me for leftovers.

Needless to say, she had ignored the fat-free, carb-free, taste-free diet food I'd sloshed in her bowl. Now she was yowling at my ankles, demanding to be fed.

"Here, honey," I said, tossing her the square of fish I'd saved her from my dinner plate.

(Trust me, it was not a sacrifice.)

She inhaled it with the speed of a Hoover, then looked up at me with hungry eyes.

So what else you got?

"I swear, Pro, that's all I have."

An outraged swish of her tail.

What??? No crab cakes?

She stalked off in high dudgeon and jumped up on top of the armoire, as far from me as she could possibly get.

Ignoring her beady glare, I climbed on my bed with my laptop.

How naïve I'd been when I'd packed it, thinking I'd be able to get started on that novel I'd always been meaning to write. I'd pictured myself working on my masterpiece stretched out on a lounge chair, a succession of papaya smoothies at my side.

Hah. There'd be no lounging around at this joint. And certainly no papaya smoothies. And how could I possibly write a novel in a state of semi-starvation?

Now I opened my computer and began composing a most reproving e-mail to Lance. I'd been calling him for the past several hours on my cell. Naturally the little weasel had been avoiding my calls (perhaps turned off by a death threat or two I may have uttered). But if he thought he was going to escape my wrath, he had another thing coming. In no uncertain terms, I told him what a stinker he was for sending me off to Diet Hell under false pretenses.

My anger spent, I then headed for the bathroom, where I intended to soak my blues away in a relaxing bubble bath.

But just as I was about to step in the tub, I was suddenly overcome by the aroma of fresh-baked vanilla cookies. Oh, dear. Was I having an olfactory mirage? Was I so hungry my mind was playing tricks on me? Or was someone actually baking a batch of cookies?

You'll be relieved to know I had not gone bonkers. Not then, anyway.

It was just those dratted bubbles!

Would you believe the bath gel Olga had chosen for her guests was something called Vanilla Cookies 'N Cream?!

A little sadistic, n'est-ce pas?

Needless to say, I promptly abandoned the tub and took a brisk shower instead, my blues fully intact. Then I got in my jammies and turned on the TV, hoping to escape in an engrossing movie.

I groaned to discover that my TV got a grand total of five stations—two of them nearly white with snow. And the gods were surely conspiring against me that night, because every station I clicked seemed to feature luscious shots of mouthwatering food!

Click. There was Paula Deen, cooking a four-cheese mac and cheese. Click. A bunch of mafiosi on *The Godfather* were eating steaming vats of spaghetti and meatballs. Click. The Kansas City steak guy was busy cutting into a succulent series of filet mignons. Even the local news was running a feature on the best handmade ice cream in the county.

Everywhere I looked, calories taunted me.

Switching off the TV in disgust, I decided to go to sleep and put an end to this whole miserable day.

I beckoned to Prozac to join me in bed, but she just glared at me from the top of the armoire.

With a sigh, I turned off the light. But sleep wouldn't come. Instead of drifting off to slumberland, I kept thinking about Paula D's mac and cheese, dripping with cheddar. Finally, unable to ignore the racket coming from my growling stomach, I snapped on the light.

This was ridiculous. Maybe I should just check out in the morning and put myself out of my misery. But then I thought about Lance losing all that money. No matter how big a rat he was for

tricking me into staying at this joint, I had to
admit he meant well. I simply couldn't walk out
and waste all that dough.

No, I was going to have to quit bellyaching,
put on my big girl panties, and do what I should
have done all along:

Sneak down to the kitchen and raid the refrigerator.

Chapter 6

The hallways were deserted when I set out on my mission. It was after eleven and everyone had turned in for the night. As I would soon discover, this was one of those Early To Bed, Early to Rise joints intended to make people healthy, wealthy, and cranky in the morning.

Creeping along in my sweatsocks to muffle any possible footsteps, I made my way past the lobby and into the dining room, where the smell of steamed fish lingered unpleasantly in the air. The room was lit with shafts of moonlight, so I easily made my way past the empty tables to the swinging door leading to the kitchen.

Checking underneath the door, I smiled to see that the kitchen light was off—which meant Operation Raid the Refrigerator could continue as planned.

I pushed open the door, my heart full of hope.

Surely Olga kept normal food on hand for her aerobics staff. Maybe I'd find some bananas or dinner rolls or possibly even some peanut butter. Lost in thoughts of a peanut butter and banana sandwich on a dinner roll, possibly washed down with a Chocolate Yoo Hoo, I was suddenly jerked from my reverie by the sight of someone sitting in the shadows at the big kitchen table.

Clearly one of my fellow inmates had beaten me to the refrigerator. Just when I was wondering who it could be (my money was on Chatty Cathy), I heard:

"What the hell are you doing here?"

Good heavens. It was Olga. I'd recognize that drill sergeant bark anywhere.

I flipped on the light, and sure enough it was the Diet Nazi, sitting fork in hand, with a Sara Lee cheesecake and a bottle of tequila.

And get this. She was eating the cheesecake straight from the tin!

Not that I haven't done the same thing myself, but I don't pass myself off as some kind of calorie crusader.

"I repeat," Olga said, her steely eyes boring into me. "What are you doing here?"

Time to put on the old tap shoes.

"I . . . um . . . was thirsty, so I came for a Diet Coke."

"Oh, please," she sneered. "I know your type. You came to raid the refrigerator."

"So what if I did?" I snapped, grouchy from hunger. "I'm starving. The last time I had a three hundred calorie dinner I happened to be in diapers. What's *your* excuse?"

I shot a withering glance at the glob of cheese-cake on her fork.

"Okay, okay," she conceded. "So I'm cheat-ing. If I let you share the cheesecake, will you promise to keep your mouth shut?"

"Absolutely!" I assured the darling woman.

My salivary glands sprang into action as she got me a fork and shoved the pie tin in my di-rection.

"Your half, my half," she said, cutting into it, and giving me what was most decidedly the smaller half.

But I didn't care. Much. It was cheesecake!

I wasted no time plowing into the creamy concoction, slathered—just the way I like it—with a thick layer of cherry goo on top.

"Want some tequila?" Olga asked, holding out the bottle.

"Er . . . no thanks. But if you've any got any Chocolate Yoo Hoo, I'll take that."

"No, I don't have any Chocolate Yoo Hoo! This is a diet spa!"

"So I see," I said, lobbing another meaningful glance at the cheesecake.

Her shoulders crumpled in defeat.

"Look, I know you think I'm a hypocrite, but you'd cheat, too, if you were as stressed out as I am."

I didn't bother to tell her I was fully capable of scarfing down a cheesecake, with or without stress in my life.

"Every year that bitch comes to The Haven and drives me crazy."

I assumed the bitch in question was Mallory.

"Making snide cracks about how I need plastic surgery. Complaining about the towels. Sending back her food every five minutes. And those damn mangoes! The woman is obsessed with the things. She's convinced they're both an aphrodisiac and a diuretic. If they're not on the set of her movies, she won't perform. Honest. She has it written into her contracts. It's the *No Mangoes, No Mallory* clause. Can you believe it?"

Indeed, it was hard to believe, I thought, sneaking a hunk of cheesecake from her side of the tin.

"I swear, if she asks me one more time if the mangoes are fresh, I'm going to strangle her."

She slapped my hand, as I reached for some of her cherry topping.

"Of course, when we were working together, she was lucky to get a stick of gum, let alone a fresh mango."

"You used to work together?" I asked.

"Years ago. We were both struggling actresses starting out at the same time. For a while, we even roomed together. But then Mallory made it big," she sighed. "And I didn't."

She paused for a healthy slug of tequila.

"So I took the only part I could get. Trophy wife to a mega millionaire. Just my luck, by the time my husband died, he'd lost all his millions. Left me saddled with debt."

As she sat there, clinging to her tequila bottle, worry lines etched in her brow, I couldn't help feeling a tad sorry for her.

"All I had was the house and my jewelry. So I sold the jewelry, paid off the debt, and started

The Haven. I did well for a while, too." She smiled at the memory. "But I'm afraid I don't have a good head for business. And after a while, the spa butterflies flitted off to other spas.

"Which is why," she said, popping two of her vitamins, "I have to put up with the Mango Monster each year."

By now, we'd polished off the cheesecake, leaving the pie tin Cascade Clean.

"I'm so sorry, Olga." And I meant it. "I hope everything works out for you."

"It will, if I can just hang on to the few customers I have left. Which reminds me. You'd better get out of here, before someone sees the light on."

"Well," I said, getting up to go, "thanks so much for the cheesecake."

"I hope you realize," she said, her gaze suddenly turning steely again, "it's the last piece you'll be seeing all week."

"Of course," I lied, fully intending to make frequent after-hours refrigerator raids. Lord only knew how many of those cheesecakes Olga kept stashed away. Only next time, I'd wait until I was sure she'd gone to bed.

But now I had to throw myself on her mercy just one more time.

"I don't suppose you could spare a teensy piece of fish for my cat," I said, doing my best impersonation of Prozac's Starving Orphan look. "She's so very hungry."

"Oh, please. That cat could live for a month off the fat in her belly."

"Honestly, Olga," I said, ignoring her zinger, "you can't imagine how the poor thing is suffering."

"Oh, all right," she said. "Just this once. But after tonight, the party's over. Everything will be under lock and key."

And as she walked over to get the fish, I saw that indeed there was a padlock on the refrigerator door. As there were on all the cabinets. So engrossed had I been in scarfing down my cheesecake, I hadn't noticed the place was locked up tighter than Fort Knox.

So much for Operation Raid the Refrigerator.

YOU'VE GOT MAIL

To: Jausten
From: Shoptillyoudrop
Subject: Exciting News!

Exciting news, honey! I'm going back to school!
Well, not full-time. I'm actually just taking one
course: History of the Aztec and Incan
Civilizations. My dear friend Lydia Pinkus arranged
for a retired professor to teach the course one
afternoon a week. And not only that, Lydia has
been gracious enough to offer her own house as a
meeting place.

(You remember, Lydia, don't you, our local librarian
and long-time president of the homeowners
association? An amazing woman; we're so lucky
to have her here at Tampa Vistas.)

Anyhow, Lydia arranged for this absolutely
marvelous course, and I decided to sign up. I
asked Daddy if he wanted to do it, but he said if he
wanted to study ancient civilization all he had to
do was hang around the clubhouse.

Well, he can scoff all he wants; I'm enjoying the
class to pieces, although I must admit, I keep
getting the Aztecs confused with the Incans. Did
you know that the Aztecs (or possibly the Incans)
invented popcorn and chocolate? Isn't that
exciting?

Must run. Daddy just came home from the hardware store and is honking his horn in the driveway. He must have forgotten his house keys again.

More later, sweetheart—

XXX

Mom

PS. Omigod. I just took a look out the window. I think I may faint. It's all too horrible. Will explain later.

To: Jausten
From: DaddyO
Subject: Bargain of the Century!

Hi, Lambchop!

You'll never guess what I just bought. A complete set of garden gnomes. They were on sale—75% off! The bargain of the century! Gosh, those little guys are cute. I've got them all over the lawn, and they're quite a sight. I bet our property values will skyrocket.

You'd think your mother would be grateful for a little gnome home improvement, but noooo. For some insane reason, she finds them unattractive. She actually called them "eyesores"! This from the woman who orders sequinned capri sets from the shopping channel. She actually wanted me to return them, and when I said, "Over my dead body," she had the nerve to say, "Don't tempt me."

Naturally I'm leaving my little gnome buddies right where they are. As soon as the raves start coming in from the neighbors, I know she'll change her mind.

Love & kisses,

Daddy

To: Jausten
From: Shoptillyoudrop
Subject: Village of the Damned

I suppose Daddy told you about those ghastly gnomes he bought for our front lawn? I can't believe it. The man goes to the hardware store for a simple hose nozzle and comes home with The Village of the Damned.

I took one look, and thought I'd go blind. The phone has been positively ringing off the hook with complaints from the neighbors.

Oh, dear. There's the doorbell. I just hope it's not the police.

XXX

Mom

To: Jausten
From: DaddyO
Subject: Outraged!

You'll never guess who just stopped by. That godawful battleaxe, Lydia Pinkus—the woman who almost had me arrested just because I refused to pay an unfair library fine.

There she was, standing on our doorstep, her lips all pursed and pruny.

"As president of the Tampa Vistas Homeowners Association," she said, "I'm here to ask you to take down those hideous lawn creatures."

With that she handed me a piece of paper, some nonsense about me being in violation of the Tampa Vistas landscaping code, and giving me thirty days to take down my gnomes.

Well, if she thinks I'm going to be intimidated by a silly slip of paper, she's got another think coming. Those gnomes aren't going anywhere. And the only "hideous creature" I intend to keep off my property is Lydia Pinkus!

Love 'n hugs from

Your outraged,

Daddy

Chapter 7

The next morning the true torture began.

I was in the middle of a heavenly dream starring me, George Clooney, and a cherry cheesecake, when someone started pounding on my door with what sounded like a sledge-hammer.

Bolting awake, I checked the clock on my nightstand.

Good heavens. It was only 5:45 AM! Even the roosters were still wiping sleep from their eyes.

I staggered out of bed to get the door and found Olga in drill sergeant mode, a whistle hanging from a lanyard around her neck.

"Nature Walk in fifteen minutes!" she announced.

Nature Walk? Was she kidding? What about breakfast??

"Don't just stand there," she said. "Start getting dressed. We're meeting in the lobby."

With that she moved down the hall and resumed her sledgehammer act.

Fifteen minutes later, I left Prozac yowling in
protest over the diet glop I'd sloshed in her
bowl and headed for the lobby, where I found
all my fellow inmates.

All except Mallory.

"Hurry up, Mallory!" Olga called up to the
second floor where Mallory's digs were apparently located.

"Be right down, sweetie," Mallory trilled from
above.

But she did not come right down. On the
contrary. Our resident prima donna kept us
waiting a good twenty minutes—twenty minutes
I could've been snuggled in bed, dreaming of
G. Clooney and cherry cheesecakes.

Meanwhile the rest of us just hung around,
cooling our heels.

Kendra, her pout in full bloom, sat cross-
legged on the floor, tapping her feet impatiently.

Harvy made himself comfy on the bottom
steps of the staircase, busily texting a message
on his cell. Somehow, in the short time we'd
been given to get dressed, he'd managed not
only to mousse his hair to perfection, but to put
together an outfit straight out of a Ralph Lau-
ren photo shoot.

Nearby, Clint passed the time with a series of
steroid-enhanced hamstring stretches while Cathy
yammered in Olga's ear about how wonderful
she felt on her new diet regime.

"Honestly," she was gushing, "I think I've lost weight already!"

Olga nodded absently, glaring up at the staircase, her jaw clenched tighter with each passing minute.

Finally, Mallory came sailing down the stairs with Armani in her arms. Both wore matching turquoise jog suits, Mallory's hoodie unzipped low enough to reveal a honker emerald pendant nestled in her cleavage.

Interesting accessory choice for a nature hike, I thought, staring down at my own Dudley Do-Right wristwatch.

"So sorry we're late," she trilled. "Armani didn't like his outfit. So I had to change him three times."

She tsked at her little charge, who graced her with a petulant yip.

"Here, Kendra," she said, shoving the dog into her assistant's arms. "You take him. He doesn't feel like walking today, so I promised you'd carry him."

"If he didn't feel like walking," Kendra scowled, "why didn't you leave him in your room?"

"Don't be silly. You know Armani doesn't wike to be awone. Do you, snoogums?" Mallory cooed.

Puh-leese. There's only so much a person can take on an empty stomach.

"Okay, everybody," Olga said, with a shrill blast of her whistle. "Let's move it."

She led the way out beyond the pool area to the wooded hills behind her property.

"Now start walking," she commanded.

"Up the hill?" I blinked in dismay at the incline in front of us. It looked awfully steep.

"Yes, up the hill! Get cracking."

Another blast of that dratted whistle and the trek began.

I regret to inform you that the slope was every bit as steep as it looked.

Within minutes, I was gasping for air, my face bathed in a fine mist of sweat.

I am, after all, a woman who gets winded running to the 7-Eleven for Oreos.

Trudging upward, I noticed that once again, The Haven's caste system was in effect. Mallory, Clint, and Harvy followed directly behind Olga—Harvy chattering about how fabulous Mallory looked in turquoise, and Mallory strolling down memory lane with Clint, reliving their good old days shooting *Revenge of the Lust Busters*.

Kendra tagged behind with the irascible Armani, who persisted in barking at every bird that had the temerity to cross his path.

And bringing up the rear were the Cellulite Twins, me and Cathy.

Cathy was still blathering about how happy she was to be at The Penitentiary (I mean, The Haven) and how she could practically feel the pounds melting away. Soon I had tuned her out, wondering instead exactly how long it would take before my lungs collapsed.

In the midst of my musings I heard Cathy say, "So what do you think, Jaine?"

Oh, hell. She'd asked me a question.

"What do I think?"

"About us being diet buddies. You know. Watching out for each other in case either of us is tempted to cheat."

Please. The only thing tempting me right then were thoughts of suicide.

"Er, sure," I found myself saying.

Oh, Lord. What had I just done? The last thing I wanted was a diet buddy. Due to a lack of oxygen to my brain, however, I'd obviously lost my powers of reasoning.

By now my heart was pounding like a bongo and sweat was gushing from every pore. Just when I thought I could not take another step without an oxygen tent, Olga gave another blast of her dratted whistle.

"Pick up the pace, you two!"

Damn. She was talking to me and Cathy. And she actually expected us to walk faster! Clearly the woman had spent her formative years training at the Marquis de Sade Military Academy.

Gasping for air like a beached guppy, I forced myself to go faster, and somehow Cathy and I managed to catch up with Kendra.

Thank heavens the exertion had shut Cathy up. It was during this blessed silence, broken only by the occasional yip from Armani, that Mallory turned back to Kendra and said, "Don't forget. We have to call Daddy today and wish him a happy birthday."

"I haven't forgotten," Kendra snipped in reply. "He's my father, too, you know."

Hello! That just about stopped me in my tracks.

"You two are sisters?" I managed to gasp.

Kendra nodded glumly, clearly the designated doormat in that relationship.

Poor Kendra, with her limp hair and grim American Gothic lips. Except for her eyes, which I now saw were a rather lovely green, she bore little resemblance to her glam sister.

Lucky Mallory got all the pretty genes.

I spent the rest of the hike simultaneously pondering the fickle nature of heredity and praying for the torture to end.

At last it did.

We finally reached the top of the hill.

Below us was an unobstructed view of the small coastal town where The Haven was located. And beyond that, the majestic Pacific. White-crested waves crashed to the shore in the silvery light of the morning sun.

"Isn't that the most beautiful sight you've ever seen?" Cathy gushed.

"It sure is," I replied, my eyes riveted—not on the Pacific— but on the bright red awning of the local pizza parlor.

I knew where I'd be going after dinner that night.

One mushroom and pepperoni pizza, coming right up.

With extra anchovies for Prozac, of course.

Dripping with sweat, I trudged back to my room to shower and change before breakfast, which was still an agonizing forty-five minutes away.

(Why I wasted time on that shower I'll never know, since I'd be sweating bullets before the morning was over.)

I was almost finished dressing when I heard a knock on the door.

I opened it to find The Haven's maid, a perky slip of a thing whose name tag read DELPHINE. Like Kevin the chef, she was probably somewhere in her late teens. A splash of freckles dotted her nose, and her shiny black hair was pulled back in a pony tail.

"I didn't realize you were still here," she said with an apologetic smile. "Should I come back later?"

"No, that's all right," I said, motioning for her to come in. "I'm almost ready to leave."

Seconds later she wheeled in a big creaky supply cart.

Prozac, who had been engaged—as she often is in times of stress—in a thorough examination of her privates, suddenly looked up from her perch on my bed, her pink nose twitching.

With meteor-like speed, she then zoomed over to the cart and started sniffing furiously at the towels on the bottom shelf.

Which, of course, had me baffled. Never once in all her years sniffing smelly sneakers and trash cans had she ever shown the slightest interest in freshly laundered towels.

"Prozac, what on earth are you doing?"

Delphine smiled serenely.

"Oh, your kitty probably smells the pastrami."

"Pastrami?"

With that, Delphine lifted a few strategically

placed towels to reveal a cornucopia of breakfast pastries, gourmet cat food, and packaged
sandwiches. One of which was the aforemen-
tioned pastrami.

My God, that sandwich looked good, I thought,
my salivary glands jolting awake.

"The pay here stinks," Delphine explained,
"so I have to do something to supplement my in-
come. I'm working my way through community
college," she added, a hint of pride in her voice.

What an enterprising little angel of mercy!

"Would you care to stock up on some goodies?" She gestured to her wares like Vanna White
revealing a vowel.

Would I ever! I came *thisclose* to throwing my
arms around her tiny waist and sobbing in gratitude.

"How much?" I asked, trying not to drool.

"Fifteen for the Danish, twenty for the Fancy
Feast, and thirty for the pastrami sandwich."

"Thirty cents for a pastrami sandwich?" I
asked.

My angel of mercy sure didn't have much of a
head for business.

"Hahahahahahaha," she trilled gaily. "Not cents.
Dollars. Fifteen bucks for the danish, twenty for
the cat food, and thirty for the sandwich."

"Thirty bucks for a pastrami sandwich?" I
blinked in disbelief.

"Five bucks extra if you want mustard."

"That's outrageous!"

"Take it or leave it," she shrugged.

By now, Prozac was frantic with desire, practically pulling the tab on the Fancy Feast can herself.

"Looks like kitty is hungry," Delphine said with a sly grin. "Perhaps she'd like some yummy lamb guts in savory sauce."

Prozac glared up at me through slitted eyes.

If these lamb guts aren't in my bowl in two minutes, yours will be.

Unwilling to face Prozac's wrath, I forked over twenty bucks for a measly can of cat food.

To this day, I still seethe when I think about it.

"How about that pastrami?" Delphine asked, waving the overstuffed sandwich in my face. "I'll give you a break on the mustard. For you, only two bucks extra."

"Forget it!" I said, for once in my life exhibiting some willpower.

"Sooner or later you'll break down," she said, tossing the sandwich back into the cart. "Your kind always does."

That last crack accompanied by a most snarky glance at my thighs.

But I wasn't about to break down. No way. I hadn't forgotten that pizza parlor in town. By the end of the day, I'd be wrapping myself around a nice juicy mushroom and pepperoni pizza.

Turning on my heel, I marched off to the bathroom where I tossed out Prozac's diet breakfast and replaced it with the treasured lamb guts. Which she dove into like a B-52 on overdrive.

Back in the bedroom, Delphine was busy

making my bed. As she bent over the sheets, her back to me, I glanced at her supply cart, just inches from my fingertips. How easy it would be to reach down and swipe that pastrami sandwich.

It would serve Delphine right, for gouging her helpless victims the way she did.

Maybe I could even grab a Danish pastry while I was at it.

I was busy trying to ignore a lecture from my conscience on how Thou Shalt Not Steal—Not Even from Demon Teens, when I heard Delphine say:

"Don't even think about it."

Good heavens. Did the little monster have eyes behind her head?

Then I realized she was looking at my reflection in the mirror above the dresser.

"I have no idea what you're talking about," I said in my frostiest voice.

Bidding her a not-so-fond adieu, I headed out the door, with the scent of pastrami still lingering in my nostrils.

"Leave me a note if you want a chocolate on your pillow tonight," she called out. "It's twenty bucks per chocolate. Twenty-five with nuts."

YOU'VE GOT MAIL

To: Jausten
From: Shoptillyoudrop
Subject: So Darn Mad!

I'm so darn mad it's not even funny! Not only hasn't Daddy gotten rid of the darn things, he's actually put up a sign on our lawn that says SAVE THE GNOMES!

Plus he just sent away for a bunch of *I ❤ MY GNOMES* boxer shorts and T-shirts. And spent a small fortune to have the stuff overnighted.

It's bad enough the little monsters are camping out on our front lawn, now they're invading the house, too!

Honestly, honey, I don't see how things could possibly get any worse.

XXX

Mom

To: Jausten
From: Shoptillyoudrop

Omigod. Things just got worse.

To: Jausten
From: DaddyO
Subject: DADDY FOR PRESIDENT!

Exciting new development in my fight to Save the Gnomes! I'm running for president of the Tampa Vistas Homeowners Association.

That's right, Lambchop. I was over the clubhouse and saw a notice announcing the upcoming elections. Lydia Pinkus is running for president just like she always does—unopposed. And right then and there I decided to throw my hat in the ring. That damn battleaxe has been president of the association for five years in a row—that's five years too long, IMHO. If you ask me, she's nothing but a despot in support hose.

True, the election's in just five days. But that's not going to stop me. No, siree. I'm entering the race as a write-in candidate, and plan to conduct a campaign that'll knock "La Pinkus" to kingdom come.

It's time Tampa Vistas had a president with vision and integrity and the courage to speak out against the plight of lawn gnomes everywhere! In other words, your very own DaddyO!

Love and kiss from,

Daddy (aka Mr. President)

PS. How's this for a campaign slogan? *Time to Get
Rid a Ya, Lydia!*

To: Jausten
From: Sir Lancelot
Subject: A Tad Miffed

Jaine, Sweetie—

I know you must be a tad miffed with me for
tricking you into staying at The Haven. But you
know I only did it because I love you and care
about you. Trust me, you'll thank me when we're
shopping for skinny jeans at Bloomie's.

Hug hug, kiss kiss,

Lance

PS. Had dinner last night at a great new Italian
restaurant on Melrose. The risotto was divine!

Chapter 8

Breakfast was a depressing affair of hot lemon water and chopped cardboard (which Olga insisted on calling cereal). As I choked it down, I felt a queasy feeling in the pit of my stomach. Partly it was from the chopped cardboard. But mainly from the e-mails I'd read when I'd gone to my room to shower and change.

Don't get me wrong. My parents are sweethearts of the highest order, and I love them to pieces. But for some reason, wherever they go, disaster seems to follow. Daddy's the main culprit, of course. This is a man who attracts trouble like white cashmere attracts wine stains. He's broken so many of the bylaws at my parents' retirement community, they've practically got his picture up at the local post office. I shuddered at the thought of him running for office on his Save The Gnomes platform.

And as for Lance, how do you like the nerve of that little weasel? Stuffing his face with risotto while I was starving in diet hell! Just wait till I get my hands on him!

But all thoughts of Lance and Daddy were interrupted after breakfast when Olga took me aside, and announced:

"Time for your weigh in!"

"My weigh in?" I gasped, beads of sweat popping up on my brow.

"It's a routine procedure. We weigh you now so you can see how much weight you've lost by the end of the week."

The last time I stepped on a scale of my own free will was, well, never. So you can imagine how upset I was.

"Can't we just make a guesstimate?" I asked. "Say, somewhere between 120 and *The Biggest Loser?*"

Olga nixed that plan in no uncertain terms and herded me over to The Haven's gym.

Like the Spa Therapy Center, the gym was a charmless box of a building, fluorescent-lit and linoleum-clad, used mainly—as my poor muscles would soon discover—for aerobics.

As we walked inside, I saw a buff young couple working out on some treadmills.

"Jaine," Olga said, gesturing to them with pride, "meet Sven and Shawna, two of my most valued employees."

Sven was a throbbing hunk of nonstop muscles and piercing blue eyes; Shawna, an equally striking blonde, with lush eyelashes and lusher lips.

Clearly these two were prominent members of the Ken and Barbie family tree.

"Sven and Shawna are both aerobics instructors," Olga explained, "as well as licensed massage therapists."

They flashed me twin Ultra Brite smiles, nearly blinding me in the process.

"Get the record book, Shawna," Olga said, snapping her fingers. "It's time for Jaine's weigh in.

I groaned to see my long-time nemesis, Mr. Detecto, the scale, lurking in a corner, along with a strange egg-shaped piece of equipment.

Shawna clambered off her treadmill and scooted off to retrieve a ledger from a small office adjacent to the gym.

"Okay, Jaine," Olga barked, pointing to the scale. "Get your fanny up there!"

"Can't I take off my shoes first? And my watch? And my scrunchy? And this tissue in my pocket—"

"On the scale!" she glowered. "Now!"

Reluctantly I stepped on the scale, holding my breath in the mistaken belief that it would somehow make me thinner.

Olga's eyebrows shot up in disapproval as she moved the weight bar over a notch or two.

"What a tub of lard!"

Okay, she didn't really say that. But what she did next was almost as bad. She shouted out my weight, all three depressing digits, in a voice that could be heard in the next county. Along with Colonel Sanders' herbs and spices, my weight happens to be a carefully guarded national secret, and I didn't appreciate her blabbing it at the top of her lungs.

Over at his treadmill, Sven had the grace to pretend he couldn't hear what was happening.

I'd barely stepped down off the scale when Olga whipped out a tape measure from one of her pockets and cinched it around my middle.

"My God, Jaine, I've measured radial tires smaller than your waist."

Okay, she didn't say that, either, but I could tell that's what she was thinking as she shouted out my measurements for Shawna to enter in the record book.

Shawna dutifully noted them down, shooting me a sympathetic smile.

Olga finished taking my measurements, making the most annoying *tsk tsk* sounds when she got to my hips. At last my ordeal was over, and I was just about to make a break for it, when she shoved her sinewy arm in my path.

"Not so fast. You still have to do the Fat Vat."

"The Fat Vat?"

"A body composition assessment machine," she said, pointing to the egg-shaped contraption I'd noticed earlier. "It measures your body fat. We call it the Fat Vat."

I now saw that it was hooked up to a computer.

Olga swung open the machine's door, revealing a bench inside.

"Go ahead. Grab a seat."

I did as instructed, and she slammed the door shut.

Good heavens, I felt like a chick about to be hatched. It was awfully close in there. And something about the air pressure made my ears start to pop. I watched through a thick glass window as Olga fiddled at the computer. Finally, after what seemed like an eternity but was probably only five highly claustrophobic minutes, she let me out.

It turns out I had a thriving colony of fat cells. A regular fat cell condo, if you will. My poor muscles were about as out of place on my bod as an Amish family in Vegas.

"We certainly have our work cut out for us, don't we?" Olga sneered.

Refusing to dignify her barb with a reply, I gathered my fat cells and started for the door, entertaining serious thoughts of Lance-o-cide.

I did not get very far, however, because just as I was leaving, the rest of the inmates came filing in for a fresh round of exercise hell.

"Welcome everybody," Sven said, flashing a blinding smile. "I'm Sven, and this is Shawna. Today we'll be leading you in your first aerobics class."

"Well, hello," said Mallory, raking her eyes over Sven's abs of steel. "Where do I sign up for private lessons?"

Sven blushed under his perfect tan.

"You must be new here," Mallory cooed.

"My wife and I started working at The Haven about two months ago," Sven managed to stammer.

"You're married?" Mallory pouted in mock disappointment.

Next to me, Kendra whispered, "That's never stopped her before."

"Yes," Shawna said, staking claim to her man. "We've been happily married for almost six years."

"Enjoy it while you can, honey," Kendra muttered.

Poor Shawna. If Mallory decided to make a play for her husband, I feared she'd be in deep doo doo. Her beach bunny good looks were worthy of a wolf whistle or three, but she was no match for the spectacular Mallory, who had shown up in bike shorts and a tight white tank top, leaving nary an inch of her bodacious bod to the imagination.

"Okay, everybody," Sven clapped his hands. "Let's get started."

He then proceeded to lead us through a series of exercises last practiced on a Viking slave ship. Before long, muscles I didn't even know I had were screeching in agony.

As Sven demonstrated the exercises, Shawna circulated among us, correcting our form.

The class had been divided into two rows, with the "A" list up front and the Untouchables in the rear. Mallory had positioned herself directly in front of Sven, where she was making sure to expose every possible inch of cleavage, her emerald pendant bouncing with each strategic jiggle.

Alongside her, Clint was breezing through the exercises on autopilot, his mind a million miles away. He probably did stuff like this in his sleep. Nor did Harvy and Kendra seem to be having any trouble keeping up. As part of Mallory's entourage, they were no doubt used to working their tails off.

Only Cathy and I were struggling. And compared to me, Cathy was an Olympic champ.

Needless to say, Shawna was spending a lot of time at my side.

"Can't you raise that leg a little higher?" she asked during one particularly hellish routine.

"Not without a forklift."

Finally, when my muscles were on their knees, begging for mercy, Sven called out, "Okay, everybody. That's it for the warm up."

The warm up?? Dear God, don't tell me there was more!

Indeed there was.

Seconds later, Shawna was passing out "exercise bars," yard-long metal poles that weighed about as much as a small refrigerator. Sven then began leading us in a whole new set of exercises, designed to torture a whole new set of muscles.

I did my best to keep up with the others, wielding the metal tube with all the skill of an asthmatic drum majorette.

By now I was looking back fondly on the old good days of the nature hike.

At last the session was over. Shawna pulled me up from where I had collapsed on the floor while everybody else filed out the door.

Everybody, that is, except Mallory, who had chosen to linger behind.

"Let me help you put these away," she said to

Sven, exposing her cleavage as she bent down to pick up her exercise bar.

For heavens sakes. Talk about shameless. Didn't she realize the man's wife was standing not two feet away?

"That's okay," Sven said, with an awkward smile. "Shawna and I can take care of it."

"Yes, we'll be fine," Shawna added, hurrying to Sven's side, a big fat phony smile plastered on her face.

But as Mallory sauntered out the door, working every inch of her mojo, I saw fear in Shawna's eyes.

And I didn't blame her. Not one bit.

Sven was staring at Mallory like a starving man at an all-you-can-eat buffet.

For Shawna's sake, I just hoped he could resist temptation.

Chapter 9

After a refreshing bottle of lukewarm water, Olga announced that it was time for our "chores."

Everyone at The Haven, she explained, was expected to pitch in and help out. Yep, that's right. Having forked over hundreds of dollars a night to stay at this joint, we were now expected to take turns mowing the lawn, pruning the bushes, and weeding the organic garden.

I blinked in disbelief.

This was nothing but slave labor. Olga just didn't want to spend money on a gardener!

Not surprisingly, when the chores were handed out, Mallory and Clint were excused and given "meditation" breaks. Olga claimed they'd get their chores later on. I could just imagine what those would be. Testing the cushions on the lounge chairs, no doubt.

The rest of us peons were put to work: Harvy

and Kendra, mowing. Cathy, pruning. And me? I got all the fun of weeding that damn organic garden.

The morning fog had long since taken a powder, and as I crouched down to begin my stint among the vegetables, I could feel the midday sun searing into my back.

Before long, I was gushing sweat like a busted fire hydrant.

I was on my knees, yanking a dandelion from between the zucchinis and making imaginary arrangements for Lance's funeral, when I heard Mallory's voice drifting from above.

I looked up at what must have been her balcony and saw that her French doors were open.

A few more beats of chatter and I realized she was talking to a man. At first I thought it was Sven, come for a little after-workout workout. What I did next was extremely tacky, but I just had to hear what was going on. So I scooted closer to the building to do a little eavesdropping.

"Care for some pinot grigio, darling?" I heard Mallory ask. "I've got some chilling in the minifridge."

So the A-listers got minifridges. How nice for them. Something told me I'd be lucky to get fresh towels.

Soon I heard a cork pop and glasses clink.

Then the man began speaking again.

"To your new book, babe."

Surprise. It wasn't Sven, after all.

No, I recognized that deep gravelly voice from a zillion movie promos. It was Clint Masters.

Good heavens. Did Mallory have her eye on Clint, too?

I sat there, waiting for the next step in this real life soap opera.

At first they were just chattering about how great it was to see each other, how 2007 was such a wonderful year for pinot grigios, and how exciting it was that Mallory was writing a memoir.

Just your usual blah blah yakety yak.

I was about to give up and creep out of hearing range, but then I heard something that piqued my interest.

"You're not really going to write about what you saw that day in my dressing room, are you?" Clint asked with a nervous laugh.

"Of course I am, darling," Mallory trilled in reply.

"But if you do," Clint said, an edge of desperation creeping into his voice, "you'll destroy my career."

"Sorry, sweetie, but nothing sells a memoir like a dishy story about a macho action hero who likes to dress up in ladies lingerie."

Holy zucchini! So Clint Masters, reigning king of the Celluloid Studs, was a cross-dresser! Now that was a newsflash destined to hit the tabloids. No wonder Clint was staying at The Haven. He hadn't come here to shape up. He'd heard about Mallory's memoir, and had come to plead his case.

"Aw, c'mon, Mallory," he whined. "I'll be ruined."

"Sweetie, you must have me confused with someone who gives a flying fig."

Of course the word she used was not *fig*, but this is a family health food novel, so I'll spare you the colorful four letters involved.

"Care for some more pinot grigio, darling?"

"No, I would not care for some more of your girlie white wine," Clint snarled.

All traces of desperation had vanished from his voice. Now he was the action hero who single-handedly beat up an entire cell of Taliban terrorists, armed only with his bare fists and a Swiss army knife.

"Trust me, Mallory," he growled, "you don't want to mess with me."

"Or what?" She laughed. "You'll pistol whip me with your mascara wand?"

The next thing I knew, I heard the sound of glass smashing.

"For God's sake, Clint," Mallory gasped. "You almost killed me with that wine bottle."

"Oh, well," Clint said. "Practice makes perfect."

Then the door slammed so hard, I wondered if it had come off the hinges.

I stood among the organic veggies, stunned.

Correct me if I'm wrong, but hadn't Clint Masters just issued a death threat?

If Mallory was upset, she showed absolutely no signs of it at lunch. She sat at the "A" table—chatting with Harvy about an upcoming photo shoot and driving Olga crazy with special requests from the kitchen—seemingly oblivious to Clint, who sat next to her stabbing his lettuce shards much like he'd stabbed those Taliban terrorists.

The hours after lunch passed in a blur of treadmills, tai chi, and aqua-cise—the latter a particularly humiliating experience. The last time I willingly exposed my thighs to the public was at childbirth.

I told Olga I hadn't brought a bathing suit, but unfortunately the Diet Nazi had a bunch of loaner suits. And soon I was squeezing myself into a black latex Mother Teresa model that made me look like a sausage in mourning.

Mallory took one look at my thighs and snickered.

"Liposuction, anyone?" I heard her whisper to Harvy.

Relief finally came when Olga gave us the rest of the afternoon off—hallelujah!—and it was time for my first massage. Truly, the highlight of my day.

Possibly, my life.

Darling Shawna, who I soon came to think of as The Miracle Worker, ushered me into a spa cubicle and proceeded to coddle me as I have never been coddled before. First she sat me down in a small wicker chair and handed me a cup of The Haven's muscle-relaxing tea—imported, as Olga had told me on her orientation spiel, all the way from Tibet and brewed in the ornate urn I'd seen out in the corridor.

"It's been steeped a full twenty minutes," Shawna explained, "to bring out all its medicinal qualities."

I shuddered to think what it would taste like.

But alert the media. It was actually quite nice. Naturally sweet and cinnamony. The best thing I'd had since last night's cheesecake.

As I savored every mouthful, Shawna began giving me the most divine foot rub, first soaking my aching tootsies in warm water, then rubbing them with soothing lavender lotion.

When she had massaged my feet to the consistency of limp linguini, she settled me on the massage table. All the while smiling serenely, showing no signs of the stress I'd seen earlier in the gym.

As tinkly sitar music played in the background, she set to work easing every kink in my knotted muscles with her magic fingers. Before long—aside from the hollow pit formerly known as my stomach—I was feeling almost human again.

Now *this* was my idea of a spa.

Just when I was wishing the massage could go on forever—with only an occasional Chunky Monkey break—I heard soft moans coming from the next cubicle.

"Oh, Sven!" an unmistakable hush puppy voice crooned. "That feels sooo wonderful!"

It was Mallory, making noises normally heard in a porn flick.

I sneaked a peek at Shawna. Aside from a tiny tic in her temple, she showed no signs of being upset.

"Does Sven usually give massages to women?" I asked.

"All the time," she replied evenly. "The gals just love him."

"So I've noticed."

"Excuse me just a minute, will you?"

With that she walked over to a CD player on her work station and cranked up the volume on the sitar music, drowning out the moans of ecstasy from the next cubicle.

Then she returned to the massage table, mission accomplished.

She'd managed to get rid of Mallory.

For the time being, anyway.

All too soon, my massage was over, and I spent the rest of the afternoon by the pool, lying dazed in a deck chair, trying to tune out Cathy as she blathered on about the merits of Paper Vs. Plastic. In case you're interested (and even if you're not): Plastic's a cinch, because you just load a whole bunch of bags on the metal holders and drop in the groceries.

But paper, on the other hand—whatever you do, don't get Cathy started on paper. That's at least fifteen minutes of your life you'll never get back. The trouble with paper is you've got to reach over and get each individual bag, and then you've got to pull it open, and heaven help you if it doesn't have handles. ("The way some customers act," Cathy huffed, "you'd think I'd just shortchanged them again.")

Of course, what really bugged Cathy were the people who wanted paper *and* plastic. ("For heavens sakes, can't they make up their mind?") According to Cathy—and you will be quizzed on this at the end of the book—the world would be a better place if customers bagged their own groceries.

Needless to say by the time dinner rolled around, I was ready to eat the wallpaper.

The wallpaper, yes. But not the depressing retread of last night's fish and veggie fiasco. Somehow Kevin the cook had managed to poach every iota of flavor from the ghastly gray blob of fish on my plate. I struggled to get down a few mouthfuls and saved the rest for Prozac.

Back in my room, I found her out on the patio, her pink nose up against the mesh screen, staring intently at a koi pond just a few yards away. As she watched the plump golden fish flitting about in the moonlight, I knew exactly what the little monster was thinking.

Bet they'd be yummy sautéed in butter sauce.

"Forget it, Pro. They're for ornamental purposes only."

Then she turned from the screen and began her patented Feed Me dance around my ankles. It had been ages since her Fancy Feast, and she was ravenous.

Hurrying to her food bowl, I tossed out the diet glop she had been ignoring, and gave her my Gray Fish ala Kevin.

Even Prozac, a world-class chow hound, sniffed at it in disdain. But she ate it anyway, and began howling for more.

"Hang in there, honey. I'm heading into town to get us some goodies."

Indeed, I had not forgotten my plan to slip into town after dinner and swan dive into a pepperoni pizza. As soon as I'd wolfed it down, I'd

pop in at the local convenience store for
Prozac's cat food, and a candy bar or three to
tide me over until the next night.

"Soon," I promised, "you'll be feasting on Savory Salmon Guts."

Prozac greeted that news with a bossy swish of
her tail.

Okay, but make it snappy!!

Bidding her a hasty adieu, I grabbed my wal-
let and car keys and headed down the hallway. I
was just about to slip past the lobby to freedom,
when Olga jumped out from nowhere.

"Oh there you are, Jaine," she said, grabbing
my elbow. "We're all waiting for you. I'm about
to begin my lecture."

Her lecture??? For crying out loud. Exercise
all day, and a lecture at night? How much could
a body stand?

She marched me into the lounge where the
other inmates were seated—Mallory and Harvy,
cozy on a loveseat; Clint and Kendra, glowering
in nearby armchairs. Only Cathy sat at the edge
of her chair, eager for the festivities to begin. I
took a seat as close to the door as possible.

As Olga trotted over to the massive fireplace
to begin her talk, I saw Mallory sneak a sip of
vodka from a minibottle.

"Tonight's lecture," Olga announced, "will be
Fun Facts About Trans Fats."

Trust me. There are no fun facts about trans
fats. Which quickly became evident from Olga's
lecture, a yawnfest that made Cathy's paper vs.
plastic dissertation seem like an HBO comedy
special.

As Olga droned on, I shook my head in disbelief. The nerve of that woman. Lecturing us on healthy eating, when just last night she was stuffing her face with Sara Lee!

At last she ran out of fun facts and the lecture ground to a halt.

Cathy asked me if I want to join her in a game of Parcheesi, but I told her I was bushed and that I was going straight to bed.

Which was a lie, of course.

I did not intend to go anywhere near my bed. Instead I snuck out the back door and over to the parking lot.

By the time I got in my car, I could practically taste the pepperoni.

Chapter 10

I groaned when I saw the sign in the pizza parlor window.

CLOSED

Darn that Olga. If only she hadn't yakked for so long, I might have made it in time.

Cursing her and her stultifying trans fat lecture, I checked out the only other restaurant on the town's tiny main street, a froufrou French joint I shall call, for the purposes of this narrative, Le Petit Ripoff. You know the kind of place. Where the prices are sky high and the customer is never right. It was still open, but I wasn't about to fork over thirty-seven bucks for a slice of duck in orange sauce.

I'd just have to make do at the local convenience store, a minimarket called Darryl's Deli.

Great news. Not only was Darryl's open, but

to my eternal gratitude, Darryl turned out to be a discerning purveyor of fine chow.

Making my way down the narrow aisles to the prepared foods section, my eyes lit up at the sight of a ham and melted Swiss cheese sandwich on a gorgeous foccacia bun. I quickly tossed it into my cart, along with a side of cold pasta salad, and several cans of assorted fish innards for Pro. For dessert, I treated myself to a pint of fudge ripple ice cream. Normally I am a Chunky Monkey gal, but after my George Clooney/hot fudge sundae fantasy, I zeroed in on the vanilla ice cream swirled with fudge. I even went a tad crazy and bought a small jar of imported fudge sauce.

My taste buds, which had been lying dazed in my mouth from the onslaught of Kevin's gray fish, suddenly sprang to life. This was gonna be even better than the pepperoni pizza.

Grabbing a few emergency candy bars, I wheeled my cart to the checkout counter where a lanky guy with shaggy hair was sitting at the register reading a book. As I got closer, I saw the book was by P.G. Wodehouse, one of my all time fave authors. How interesting.

"Welcome to Darryl's Deli," he said. "I'm Darryl."

God, what a great smile—the kind I'm a sucker for—with deep laugh lines around the edges.

Suddenly I was conscious of my baggy sweats and grungy mop of curls.

"You must be from The Haven," he said.

Oh, crud. What if Darryl's Deli had some sort of deal with Olga? What if he refused to sell food to customers cheating on their diets?

"Yes, I'm staying there," I said, waiting for an alarm to go off and the Calorie Cops to come racing in and drag me back to Diet Hell.

But thank heavens he just started ringing up my sale.

"I figured you must be," he said. "I know pretty much everybody in town, and if you lived here, I would have remembered you."

There was that smile again. Was it my imagination, or was this guy flirting with me?

Oh, why the heck hadn't I at least put on some lipstick?

"I get a lot of customers from The Haven. I hear the food stinks."

"Straight out of *Oliver Twist*."

"You poor kid."

At last. Someone who understood my pain.

"Excellent choice," he said, holding up the fudge sauce. "I see you're a connoisseur of fine chocolate."

Needless to say, I didn't tell him that when it came to chocolate, I'd eat anything that wasn't nailed to the shelf.

"Well," he said, as he started to bag my stuff, "enjoy all your goodies."

I looked down at the giant sandwich, the cole slaw, the ice cream, the fudge sauce, the candy bars and a Hershey's Kiss I'd tossed in for good measure, and suddenly I was embarrassed. I did not want Darryl to think I was the kind of gal who could polish off this cholesterol festival all by herself. Of course I *am* that kind of gal, but I didn't want him to think it.

Which is the only explanation I can offer for what I said next.

"Oh, but this isn't for me."

"It isn't?"

"No," I said with a carefree wave. "It's for my roommate."

He held up a can of cat food. "Your cat eats cole slaw?"

"Not my cat. My other roommate. My, um, my grandmother. Yes. Grammy Austen. Darling Grammy. Such a sweetie. She taught me how to crochet my first potholder when I was five!"

Oh, hell. Where was this stuff coming from? The real Grammy Austen is a kamikaze bingo player raising hell in her assisted living home in Altoona, PA. And the only thing she ever taught me was how to make a good martini.

"Anyhow," I babbled, "the doctors wanted Grammy to lose some weight, so here we are. But the food at The Haven was so horrible, Grammy got the munchies and begged me to run into town for a snack. And I just couldn't say no."

Did I detect a hint of a smile on those killer lips?

"Well, I hope she gives you a bite of the sandwich. I made the bread myself."

"You did?"

"I cook a lot of food for the store. You should try my cannelloni."

Wow. Not only cute, but a cook, too!

"Nice meeting you," he said, handing me my grocery bag. "And give my best to your grandmother."

"Oh, I will."

"And come back soon."

No doubt about that.

I skipped out of the store with a song in my heart and a Hershey's Kiss in my mouth.

True, I'd told that wee fib about Grammy Austen, but who cared? The bottom line is: I'd had a close encounter with a cannelloni-cooking cutie and I'd scored some fabulous chow.

At last lady luck had returned to my side.

But not, alas, for long.

Guess who was waiting for me when I came skipping up the path to The Haven with my goodie bag? Those of you who guessed "George Clooney," go straight to the back of the class and put on your dunce cap.

It was the Diet Nazi, of course. Olga stood glowering in the open door, arms clamped across her chest.

"Give it to me," she said, holding out her hand for my goodies.

I peeked into my shopping bag and saw my glorious ham and Swiss beckoning to me, the ice cream and fudge sauce calling my name.

For a second I was tempted to dash back to the car and lock myself in, defying the Diet

Nazi. What could she do to me—have me arrested for snacking?

But before I could act on my impulse, Olga had snatched the bag from my hand.

"How could you?" she said, holding up an Almond Joy.

I saw the way she was eyeing that candy bar. Whaddaya bet she'd be scarfing it down the minute she was alone?

By now Cathy had wandered into the lobby in her bathrobe and pajamas, taking in the scene.

"I offered to be her diet buddy," the little stoolie piped up.

"That was very generous of you, Cathy." Olga shot her a Good Cop smile. "Now let's all go to bed and pretend this shameful affair never happened."

Cathy headed back upstairs to her room, having the nerve to actually smile at me and say, "Don't feel bad, Jaine. I'll be there for you next time."

"Just leave me alone and worry about your own damn cellulite," were the words I was too polite to utter as I turned on my heel and marched back to my room.

I was just about to let myself in, when I saw Delphine wheeling her cart out of a supply closet across the hall.

"What are you still doing here?" I asked.

"Waiting for you," the perky teenager replied. "I saw what happened just now. I knew you'd try your little stunt." She nodded smugly. "Your kind always does."

This kid was really beginning to get on my nerves.

"So, how about it?" she asked. "Ready to do business?"

She gestured to the bottom shelf of her cart, where all her groceries were stashed.

"No, thank you. I'd rather go hungry than submit to your kind of extortion."

Okay, so I didn't really say that.

The lily-livered words that actually came out of my mouth were:

"Do you take credit cards?"

Delphine didn't take credit cards, but she did take checks. And just my rotten luck I had enough in my account to cover her exorbitant prices.

I would have loved nothing better than to write that freckle-faced thief a rubber check.

"So what'll be?" she asked, wheeling her cart into my room.

Prozac leaped off her treadmill from where she'd been napping, and came charging over to Delphine.

I don't know about her, but I'll take one of everything.

"I'll have a pastrami sandwich," I said, remembering the menu from earlier that day. "And a couple of Fancy Feasts. And an Almond Joy if you've got one."

"Sorry," Delphine shrugged. "I'm out of pastrami. All I've got left is American cheese."

She held out a plain American cheese sandwich. And I do mean plain. No lettuce, no tomato, no nothing.

"How much?" I asked.

"Thirty-five bucks."

"But just this morning the pastrami was only thirty."

"You snooze, you lose. I've raised my prices since then."

Indeed she had. The cat food, which had been twenty bucks earlier that day, was now twenty-five. And she didn't have any Almond Joy, only a dubious looking packet of candy imported from China called M&N's. For which she was charging a staggering seventeen dollars.

I seethed as I wrote out the check.

"Sure you don't want to get a six pack of cat food?" Delphine offered, holding out some more cans. "I'll give you a price break. Just one hundred bucks."

"No, thank you."

And this time I meant it. I fully intended to go back to town the next day. Only I wouldn't be foolish enough to come trotting home toting grocery bags. Somehow I'd manage to smuggle my loot into the room, even if I had to sew the stuff into my panties.

"Nighty nite," Delphine chirped, "and *bon appetit!*"

Then she wheeled her cart into the hallway, ponytail swishing.

It was all I could do not to run after her and yank the darn thing from her scalp.

I left Prozac inhaling her Fancy Feast and headed out to dine al fresco on the patio. Plopping down on the chaise, I unwrapped my sorry excuse for a sandwich. It was even worse than it looked in the wrapping—the bread stale and the cheese brittle around the edges.

The Earl of Sandwich was probably rolling over in his grave.

Still starving after only nine hundred calories and a Hershey's kiss, I ate it anyway, washing it down with a piquant vintage of bathroom tap water.

I was sitting there, gnawing on my emery board bread and rubber cheese, wishing I'd forked over the extra two bucks Delphine had demanded for a mustard packet, when suddenly I heard giggling.

I looked up and saw Mallory running up the path from the pool, her fabulous body parts jiggling in a micro bikini.

And she was not alone.

Seconds later, Sven came chasing after her in a Speedo that left little to the imagination.

Mallory smiled slyly and let herself be caught.

Sven spun her around in his arms and the next thing I knew they were locked in what can only be described as a For Mature Audiences Only embrace.

Oh, dear. So Sven hadn't been able to resist temptation, after all.

As they both ran toward The Haven, I saw someone step out from the bushes into the light from the footpath.

Good heavens. It was Shawna.

The fear I'd seen on her face in the gym, the serene smile in the spa cubicle—all gone. Now the only thing shining in her eyes was fury.

"Damn that bitch," I heard her mutter as she stormed off into the night.

YOU'VE GOT MAIL

To: Jausten
From: Shoptillyoudrop
Subject: The Death of Me Yet

Your father will be the death of me yet. Now he's decided to run for president of the homeowners association. Against Lydia Pinkus, of all people!

What's worse, he's named me his campaign manager. Which is just a nicer word for *slave*. The man has been driving me crazy. He decided to campaign door to door and hand out cookies in his new *To Gno-Me is To Love Me* T-shirt. And get this. He expected me to make miniature gnome cookies! With costume icing and everything. Who does he think I am—Martha Stewart? I told him he'd get plain old chocolate chip, and like it.

I baked him three dozen Toll House cookies which lasted him all of about seventeen minutes. That impossible man wound up eating most of them himself. He came back home with a terrible tummy ache, which served him right. In fact, I was hoping the whole experience would make him call off his candidacy, but no such luck. He woke up after a nice nap, fit as a fiddle and raring to go.

Now he's out in the garage painting a campaign sign. Would you believe he actually wanted to use the slogan, *Time to Get Rid a Ya, Lydia!* I told him if he did, he could meet me in divorce court. Well, he finally backed down and promised he'd come up with something else.

Anyhow, what with all the fuss and bother of Daddy's campaign, I haven't even had a chance to go over my notes for my Aztec and Incan History course. Oh, well. It will be a treat just to get out of the house and away from Campaign Headquarters.

Love from your frazzled,

Mom

To: Jausten
From: Shoptillyoudrop
Subject: Thought I'd Die

I just got back from class, and I swear I've never been so humiliated in all my life. There we were in Lydia's living room as our marvelous teacher, Professor Rothman, told us the most fascinating story about how the Incans (or possibly the Aztecs) invented freeze dried food, when suddenly we heard someone shouting over a bullhorn, "Save the Gnomes! Vote for Hank!"

Needless to say, that "someone" on the bullhorn was Daddy.

"Good heavens!" Lydia cried, jumping up out of her seat. "What is that man up to now?"

Then she raced over to her front window to look outside. Unfortunately everyone else followed her, so they all got to witness my humiliation.

There was Daddy in his Camry, shouting through a bullhorn as he drove, one of his godawful gnomes attached to the top of the car.

And the worst part—the very worst part—was the huge banner he had on the side of the Camry. In big bright red letters was his new campaign slogan:

PINKUS STINKS!

Honestly, honey, I thought I'd die.

I apologized profusely to Lydia, but she just took me in her arms and hugged me, saying, "You poor thing. You have to live with him."

And I could see that everyone in the room agreed with her. Professor Rothman even took me aside and gave me the name of a colleague of his, a psychiatrist, and urged me to book an appointment for Daddy ASAP.

"Meds might help," he whispered.

Needless to say, I didn't hear a word of the lecture after that.

I was so unhappy I couldn't even begin to eat the homemade lemon tarts Lydia served after class.

Well, technically, I did manage to force down a few mouthfuls. In fact, I might have finished off the whole slice, but I tell you, honey, I could barely taste a thing.

I was way too furious.

Just wait till your father gets home.

XXX

Mom

To: Jausten
From: DaddyO
Subject: Deserted!

You're not going to believe this, Lambchop, but for some crazy reason, your mom has quit as my campaign manager.

My own wife, deserting me in my hour of need! All because of an innocent little campaign sign.

But fear not! I can win this battle on my own. I am nothing if not self-reliant.

You know my motto: When the Going Gets Tough, the TOUGH—OH, DAMN, THE CAP LOCK KEY IS STUCK AGAIN. GOTTA GO GET YOUR MOM TO FIX IT.

TO BE CONTINUED—

DADDY (AKA "MR. PRESIDENT")

To: Jausten
From: Sir Lancelot
Subject: Babaganoush To Die For

Sorry I missed your calls, sweetie. All eight of
them. Crazy day. Had dinner at a new falafel place
in Westwood. The babaganoush was to die for!

Hug hug, kiss kiss,

Lance

Chapter 11

Unaccustomed to a snack-free diet, Prozac clawed me awake the next morning at some ungodly hour, yowling at the top of her lungs to be fed.

"Prozac, please," I groaned. "Show me some mercy."

But all she showed me was her little pink throat as she kept on yowling, kicking it up a notch for good measure.

Reluctantly I tore myself out of bed and staggered to the bathroom to open one of Delphine's twenty-five dollar cans of cat food, every muscle in my body throbbing from yesterday's brutal exercise regimen.

The minute the Fancy Feast hit her bowl, Prozac dove in, inhaling it—according to my lightning calculations—at about two bucks a bite.

Rubbing sleep from my eyes, I hobbled over to the French doors to check the weather.

The sun was just beginning to illuminate the sky, and like yesterday, everything was blanketed in a thick early morning fog.

I stood there, rubbing my aching calves and thinking about the e-mails I'd been foolish enough to read last night before climbing into bed. I cringed at the thought of Daddy in his *Pinkus Stinks* Gnome-Mobile. No wonder Mom quit as his campaign manager.

But Mom's anger was nothing compared to how steamed I was at Lance. Can you believe that guy? Sending me off to diet boot camp while he stuffed his face with babaganoush!

Just as I was thinking how much I'd give to baba his ganoush, I happened to see a most unusual sight—a nearly-naked man streaking out from The Haven's back door.

In spite of the fog, I knew it was Sven. I could tell by his Speedo.

Looked like somebody had spent the night burning mattresses with Mallory.

Once again, my heart went out to Shawna. Her marriage had hit a speed bump, all right. But I didn't have time to commiserate, because by now Olga was hammering on my door, yelling at me to get dressed for the nature hike.

A new day's agony was about to begin.

But I didn't care. I'd made up my mind to break out of diet prison. Yes, indeedie. It was time to take off my big girl panties and call it quits. As much as I hated to see Lance's money go to waste, I planned to check out that afternoon. Just as soon as I had one more heavenly massage from Shawna.

Once my muscles had been pampered to mush, I'd pack my bags and be winging my way back to L.A. With a pit stop at Mickey D's, of course.

Out in the lobby, Kendra informed us that Mallory was not coming on the nature hike.

"Why on earth not?" Olga asked.

"She says she's too tired."

Of course she was tired. Who wouldn't be after a night of sexcapades with Sven and his Speedo?

And the galling thing was that Olga didn't voice a single objection. If I'd tried a stunt like that, she'd be dragging me out of bed by my ears. She obviously had a separate set of rules for Princess Mallory. Or maybe she was just happy to be rid of her.

We started our trek up Mt. Olga, and in no time I was wheezing like a busted radiator. Everybody else seemed to be dragging their heels, too. Everybody except Cathy. Still gunning for the role of Diet Nazi's pet, she plastered a bright smile on her face as she huffed up the slope.

"C'mon, everybody," Olga barked, with a deafening blast of her whistle. "Let's step up the pace! What's wrong with you people today?"

"Some stupid cat woke me at the crack of dawn," Clint grunted. "That's what's wrong. The damn creature was yowling like a banshee."

"I know," Harvy said, suppressing a yawn. "I heard it, too."

"Me, too," Kendra chimed in.

"That must've been Jaine's cat, Xanax," Olga pointed out, just in case they wanted to form a lynch party later.

"Her name is Prozac," I managed to gasp between wheezes.

"Whatever," Olga said, completely uninterested in what I'd chosen to name my beloved pet. "All I know is she needs to lose weight. I hope you're making her use that treadmill."

I wisely refrained from mentioning that the only thing Pro had been using it for was to catch up on her naps.

"Oh," Cathy piped up, "so that's *your* cat I've seen out on the patio scratching the furniture."

Great. First the little fink acted shocked over my goodie bag, and now she was ratting out Prozac.

"You scratch it, you replace it!" Olga happily informed me.

"I wanted to bring my cat, Mr. Muffin," Cathy said, "but he gets so cranky when he travels."

"He couldn't be worse than her little monster," Clint snarled.

Well! I wouldn't be going to any more of *his* movies, that's for sure.

Eventually we made it up the hill and back down again with our lungs still intact.

Cathy stayed glued to my side throughout the whole ordeal, renewing her pledge to be my diet buddy, jabbering about Mr. Muffin and his crush on the neighbor's Rottweiler.

"It's so adorable the way he's always running next door to play with her!" Cathy gushed.

I'll bet he was. Even a Rottweiler had to be more fun than a Cathy chat-a-thon. Ten to one, Mr. Muffin was having the locks changed as we spoke.

The rest of the morning passed in a blur of sweat, pretty much a carbon copy of yesterday's exercise hell.

Mallory showed up for our aerobics class, once more dressed to seduce, practically doing a pole dance with her exercise bar and lingering behind afterward—no doubt to set up a rendezvous with Sven. All the while, Shawna smiled serenely, as if she had no idea about the whoopsie doodle fest going on between the two of them.

After aerobics, I headed off for a fun session of slave labor in the garden (it was my turn to prune the hedges).

Like I said, just another day on the chain gang.

Until lunch, that is.

That's when all hell broke loose.

Lunch started out peacefully enough. Mallory was at the "A" table yammering about Mallory, Cathy was at the "B" table yammering about Cathy, and I was lost in a George Clooney Chocolate Éclair Fantasy.

But it soon became obvious that Mallory was in an extra-picky mood.

"Olga dear," she said, holding out her water glass. "My water's lukewarm. It needs ice."

Olga nodded with a brittle smile and took away the offending glass. Seconds later, she trotted out from the kitchen with a glass studded with ice cubes.

Mallory waved her away.

"Oh, that's way too many!" she said. "I wanted a few cubes, hon. I didn't want to build an igloo."

Swallowing her annoyance, Olga once again went back to the kitchen.

I was beginning to think Mallory didn't really care about the water, that she was just playing with Olga. The smile on her face told me she was getting her jollies sending her former show biz colleague back and forth to the kitchen.

"How's this?" Olga asked, having returned from the kitchen with yet another glass of water.

Mallory eyed it critically.

"It's not tap water, is it?"

"Nope, it's Evian, just like you always drink."

"I can taste the difference, you know."

She took a sip and wrinkled her nose.

"You forgot the lime wedge."

It was with Herculean effort that Olga managed to restrain herself.

Her jaw clenched tight, she headed back to the kitchen and soon returned with a lime wedge on a plate.

"Thanks, sweetie," Mallory said, as Olga slammed the plate down on the table.

Just like a cat letting a mouse scamper away only to pounce again, Mallory waited until Olga was at the kitchen door before calling out, "On second thought, honey, I think I'd rather have an iced tea."

"Now you want iced tea?" Olga asked.

"Yes, sweetie. With a slice of mango."

Olga stood there, shoulders rigid. I could practically see wisps of steam coming from her ears. For a minute I was convinced she was about to explode. But no, she just stormed into the kitchen and minutes later, came out with Mallory's iced tea.

By now, we were all caught up in the drama playing out before us, waiting to see how long Mallory would continue this obnoxious game.

Olga handed Mallory her iced tea. Mallory picked up the mango slice and wrinkled her teeny nose.

"Are you sure the mango's fresh?"

And then, at long last, the volcano erupted. This was the mango that broke the camel's back.

"Of course, it's not fresh, you nitwit!" Olga snarled. "It's out of season!"

Well, whaddaya know? Someone had actually dared to cross Princess Mallory. What on earth would the demanding diva do now?

(Call for a public flogging, was my guess.)

"Excuse me," Mallory said, with forced calm. "I must've heard wrong. Did you just call me a nitwit?"

"Yes, I did." Olga clamped her arms across her chest in defiance. "And I meant every syllable. I am sick and tired of you treating me like your personal slave and catering to your every

whim, especially your insane fixation with mangoes."

Fire flashed in Mallory's eyes.

"Who the hell do you think you're talking to?"

"A certified lunatic, that's who! Every crew
you've ever worked with hates you. You know
what they call *Mad About Mallory* behind your
back? *Mad* AT *Mallory!*"

"That's not true!" Mallory huffed.

"You bet it is. You drive everybody nuts with
your mango mania! If it weren't for you and
your damn mangoes," Olga ranted, spittle flying
from her mouth, "that poor assistant director
down in Mexico would've never gotten into that
horrible accident."

"It's not my fault Pablo crashed the car!" Mallory cried. "He was a lousy driver!"

"Of course it was your fault!" Olga snapped.
"You made him drive out in a hurricane to buy
your damn mangoes, you self-centered bitch!"

By now heads were swiveling back and forth
like spectators at a tennis match. At the "A"
table, Clint was eyeing Mallory with undisguised
loathing. And here among the peasants, Kendra
wasn't bothering to hide her glee. If she could
have, I'm sure she would've been waving a "Go,
Olga!" pennant. Only Harvy seemed to show
any sympathy for his boss, tsking and patting
Mallory's hand.

But Mallory had had quite enough.

"I'm outta here," she said, shoving back her
chair. "The only reason I come to this dump
every year is because I feel sorry for you."

"Oh, please," Kendra muttered. "She hasn't felt sorry for anybody but herself in decades."

"This place is a joke!" Now on a rant of her own, Mallory waved dismissively at her surroundings. "The carpets are threadbare, the walls are dingy and the damn silverware is mismatched."

Cathy began checking her silverware.

"And you?" Mallory eyed Olga with scorn. "You're the biggest joke of all! Everybody knows you eat the candy you confiscate."

(See? I told you so!)

For the first time Olga looked taken aback. Which just fueled Mallory's fire.

"Your special herb tea, imported from Tibet?" she sneered. "Oh, it's imported all right, all the way from Costco!" She turned to the rest of us. "And that "vitamin" bottle she keeps in the kitchen? Filled with nothing but Valium!"

Next to me, Cathy gasped in surprise.

And I must admit, I was a tad shocked myself. I remembered the pills Olga swigged down in the kitchen on my orientation tour. I never dreamed she'd been popping Valium.

"You're a disgrace to the spa industry," Mallory sniffed, scooping up Armani from his bowl of chicken tenders, "and I intend to tell everyone I know just what a hellhole this place is."

Then she stalked out in high dudgeon, Armani giving an angry yip of disapproval in her wake.

"Omigosh," Cathy whispered. "Wait'll the gang at the Piggly Wiggly hears about this."

Chapter 12

I was sprawled out on the pool deck later that afternoon, after a particularly agonizing Tae Bo class. Tae Bo, for those of you not familiar with it, is a kind of cardio-boxing exercise, whose Chinese name, properly translated into English, means, "Holy shi-tzu! What just snapped?"

As I lay there, collapsed on a lounge chair, gasping for breath and begging my muscles to forgive me, I thought back to the verbal slugfest I'd witnessed at lunch.

Quel cat fight. Olga had definitely scored points with her "certified lunatic" zinger, not to mention that shudder-worthy story about Mallory sending out some poor guy to buy mangoes in a hurricane. But Mallory had struck back with a vengeance. That final threat to trash The Haven seemed to have really rattled Olga.

Oh, well. I'd soon be out of this "haven" of bad food and clashing egos.

I was lying there, counting the milliseconds till my massage with Shawna, when Cathy—resuming her ongoing role as a barnacle on my side—plopped down on the chair next to me, weighing in on the brouhaha at lunch. Frankly, she confessed, she was a bit disillusioned. She'd been saving all year for this trip, only to discover that Olga, her diet idol, was a pill-popping binge eater. And Mallory had been right about the place needing a facelift. Why, the towels in her room were so thin, they were practically see-through! On the other hand, she rattled on, she *had* lost two and a half pounds, and that's all that really mattered, wasn't it?

This internal debate would have no doubt assumed filibuster proportions, but just then Mallory came sauntering to the pool with her posse. At first I'd been shocked to see her show up for the afternoon activities. I'd thought for sure she'd have checked out after her dramatic exit at lunch. But then, during Tae Bo class, I heard her tell Harvy the only reason she was sticking around was because she was desperate to drop five pounds for her upcoming photo shoot.

She and Harvy and Kendra now took seats a few chairs down from us.

"Hi, gals!" she called out with a cheery wave, eager to disprove Olga's description of her as a "certified lunatic."

And it was working. With Cathy, anyway.

"I don't care what Olga says about her," Cathy whispered, waving back with gusto. "She seems like a perfectly lovely person to me."

"A perfectly lovely person?" I blinked in amazement.

"True, she might be a bit demanding."

A bit demanding??? Try Idi Amin with hair extensions.

"But still, it was very sweet of her to give me that autographed cocktail napkin," Cathy maintained, ever the star-struck fan.

Mallory untied the sash on her spa robe, revealing her amazing bikini-clad bod. For the life of me, I couldn't figure out where she was going to round up those five pounds she wanted to lose.

"Damn," she said, rummaging in the pocket of her robe. "I forgot my cell phone.

"Kendra," she snapped at her sister, "let me use yours."

"I didn't bring mine either." Kendra shrugged.

"Why the hell not?"

"Because I *thought* I'd be relaxing," she said, and went back to the *Cosmo* she'd been reading.

"I hope you brought yours, hon." Mallory turned to Harvy, who was seated on her other side.

"Sure thing, Mall." He handed her his lime green designer phone.

"Thank God I can count on someone around here," Mallory said, shooting Kendra a dirty look.

But Kendra just kept her eyes glued to her *Cosmo*.

"Okay," Mallory announced. "Time to send out a tweet about what a dump this place is."

It looked like she was going to live up to her threat to badmouth The Haven.

"Let's see," she mused. "What should I say? I know! *My dog's eating better than I am.*"

I couldn't argue with that.

"Oh, wait. How about this? *I've had better service at the post office!*"

"Good one!" Harvy gushed, right on cue.

"Oh, this is going to be fun," Mallory giggled, snapping open Harvy's phone. "Olga's about to lose the few customers she has left."

I was sitting there thinking maybe I hadn't been quite fair to Idi Amin in my earlier comparison, when Mallory let out a bloodcurdling scream.

"Oh, my God!" she gasped, staring down at Harvy's phone in shock.

"Wish U were here at lunch," she read aloud from the screen. "Olga told off The Mad Cow!"

She looked up at Harvy, her face flushed with fury. If anything, she was even angrier than she'd been with Olga.

"Is that what you call me?" she sputtered. "The Mad Cow???"

Harvy paled under his spray tan.

"That must be a typo, hon. You know I'm crazy about you."

He reached over to get his phone back, but she slapped his hand away and began scrolling down his recent texts.

"The Mad Cow is driving me nuts." "If I have to eat one more mango, I swear I'll strangle her." "Can't wait to kiss the bitch good-bye."

Mallory rose from her chaise and glared down at Harvy, who by now was a quivering puddle of fear.

"If you think I'm financing your salon," she hissed, "think again, mister. Time to find yourself another cow to milk."

Then she turned to Kendra.

"Call the bank, and stop payment on his check."

And for the second time that day, she stalked off in a huff.

But not before hurling Harvy's phone into the pool.

Harvy was in an advanced state of panic.

"Kendra, sweetheart," he pleaded, kneeling beside her lounge chair, "please don't call the bank. Give me a chance to make things up with Mallory."

"That should take a minor miracle," Kendra replied, rolling her eyes.

"I know!" Harvy's face lit up with hope. "I'll tell her the messages weren't mine. That someone was using my phone without my knowledge. I don't suppose you'd be willing to take the fall and say you did it? She already knows you hate her."

"Forget it, Harvy. I'm not about to be written out of her will."

"Just give me some time," Harvy begged. "I'll think of something."

"Okay, but only until tomorrow. I can't put it off any longer than that."

Harvy was sitting on his haunches, cursing the "idiot" who first invented the cell phone, when Shawna came hurrying out to the pool.

"Okay, people," she said, clapping her hands. "It's time for your seaweed wraps!"

"Seaweed wraps?" I frowned. "What about our massages?"

"No massages today," Shawna smiled brightly. "It's Seaweed Wrap Day."

Oh, foo. I'd suffered through another round in exercise hell just to be wrapped in kelp?

"You're going to love it," Shawna assured me, seeing the look of disappointment on my face.

"Better than the massage?"

"Much better than the massage. It's what everybody comes here for."

Oh, what the heck. I'd give it a shot.

(A mistake of monumental proportions. But of course, I didn't know that then.)

Shawna explained that in the interests of efficiency she'd be giving all of us our wraps at the same time.

A half hour later, she'd set us up assembly-line style in adjacent cubicles in the Spa Therapy Center.

I was assigned to the first room at the front of the hall. Mallory, still fuming from the L'Affaire Cell Phone, stormed in to the cubicle next to mine, ignoring Harvy's pleas to grant him just a few minutes to worm his way back into her good graces.

On other side of Mallory was Kendra, and down at the end of our row was Cathy.

Harvy was ushered into a cubicle across the

hall. And Clint Masters was nowhere to be seen, having opted to stay in his room and take a nap instead.

(In a silk teddy, no doubt.)

Shawna settled us each in our cubicles with a cup of The Haven's special muscle-relaxing tea, imported all the way from either Tibet or Costco and steeped a full twenty minutes in the urn in the hallway.

I sipped my tea, wearing nothing under my spa robe except a pair of The Haven's disposable paper panties, and immediately felt the tension begin to drain from my body. Who cared if Mallory was right and Olga bought the tea at Costco? The stuff really worked.

When it was my turn to be wrapped, I took off my robe, grateful the lights were dim and there were no security cameras around to record my hips for posterity. I hopped up on the massage table, which had been covered with an electric blanket and topped off with a sheet of plastic. Draping a decorous towel over my erogenous zones, Shawna began exfoliating my skin with a pair of special exfoliating gloves. (On sale in The Haven's gift shop for an outrageous twenty dollars a pair.)

Once I was smooth as a freshly sanded two-by-four, she went over to her supply table and brought back a bowl of appalling green guacamole-like goo. Which, Shawna explained, was pureed seaweed. Soon she was slathering the stuff all over my body.

Much to my surprise, I found the whole process marvelously soothing. The green goo had been heated so it slid into my freshly-exfoliated pores like Velveeta melting on an English muffin.

So mellow was I that I didn't even mind when Shawna took two slimey strands of bull kelp from the vat in the corner and crossed them over my body. And when she wrapped me in plastic and cocooned me in the warm electric blanket, I practically swooned in ecstasy.

Shawna had not led me astray.

This was *much* better than the massage.

Dimming the lights, she left me to marinate while she worked her magic on my fellow inmates. With seaweed goo melting in my pores and soft music tinkling in the background, I felt my eyelids grow heavy, and within minutes I'd drifted off into a deep sleep.

Before long I was in the middle of a heavenly dream starring me, George Clooney, and a vat of guacamole. But then, just as George was whispering sweet nothings in my ear, he started screaming at the top of his lungs.

Oh, crud. He must've gotten a good look at my thighs.

His screams grew louder and louder, and frankly I was beginning to get a bit ticked off. Okay, so he was a major motion picture star. And I was just a Weight Watchers dropout. But a girl's got feelings, you know.

Then suddenly I realized it wasn't George screaming, but a woman.

And Holy Moses. It wasn't a dream.

Those screams were real!

I sat up with a jolt, and indeed the voice I

heard was Shawna's, wailing from Mallory's cubicle next door.

Unwrapping myself from my kelp cocoon, I jumped down off the massage table, my legs wobbly from my nap. Draped in a towel, I hurried out to the corridor, leaving a trail of green goo behind me.

Shawna was standing in the doorway of Mallory's cubicle, still screaming at full throttle.

And with good reason.

As I peered over Shawna's shoulder, I saw Mallory lying naked on her massage table, eyes bulging, mouth gaping, strangled with a hunk of bull kelp.

Chapter 13

I was grief-stricken. Desolate.

Not over Mallory's death. Which was sad, of course. She was, after all, a human being. Almost.

What had me in a dither was what the sheriffs said when they showed up after the murder. After gathering all the inmates into the lounge, they told us no one was to leave town for the next few days.

Oh, crud. Just when I'd been on the brink of freedom. Why hadn't I made my escape when I had the chance?

Apparently I wasn't the only one who'd fallen asleep during the seaweed wrap. Everyone else had conked out, too. The cops suspected that our special muscle-relaxing tea had been tampered with, so there'd be no witnesses to the murder. No wonder I'd felt so mellow the minute I started drinking it. The stuff had been laced with sedatives.

And right away I flashed on the jumbo bottle of Valium sitting on Olga's kitchen table. Thanks to Mallory's rant at lunch, everyone knew it was there. Anybody could have grabbed a fistful of pills and slipped them into the tea while it was steeping in the corridor.

Soon the cops had set up headquarters in the dining room, and started calling us in for questioning.

Olga was up first. And as the Diet Nazi marched off to her interrogation, I couldn't help but think of that ugly scene at lunch and Mallory's threat to ruin The Haven. Had Olga strangled the demanding diva to keep her business afloat? She sure had the biceps for it.

Then, as I looked around at the others, I realized they all had motives to kill Mallory. Harvy, sitting on a settee with Kendra, was trying his best to look grief stricken, but the minute the cops were gone, his first words of mourning to Kendra were, "You're not going to stop payment on my check, are you?"

"No, of course not," she said, shooting him a funny look. I wondered if she was thinking what I was thinking: That maybe Harvy had bumped off The Mad Cow to save his salon.

Then again, Kendra might very well be the killer herself. Just that afternoon she'd said she was in Mallory's will. Maybe she got tired of being her sister's lapdog, and decided to cash in on her inheritance.

Clint Masters had joined us, looking quite refreshed from his "nap." Like Harvy, he'd given a halfhearted performance of a grieving friend for the cops. But now that they'd left, he was on the phone with his agent, yakking excitedly about an upcoming movie deal.

Gone was the haunted look I'd seen in his eyes. With Mallory dead, no one (except maybe the friendly folks at Frederick's of Hollywood) need ever know about his penchant for ladies' underlovelies.

Rounding out our crew of suspects was Cathy, who was parked at my side as usual. But for once, she wasn't bubbling with happy chat. Mallory's murder seemed to have put the fear of God in her.

"Omigosh," she moaned, eyes darting around the lounge. "One of you is a killer!"

"Oh, please," Kendra said. "Mallory had an enemies list as long as her hair extensions. Maybe the cook killed her. Or the maid. Or the masseuse. Especially the masseuse. Everyone could see Mallory was making time with her husband."

She was right, of course. Who's to say Shawna hadn't strangled Mallory herself and then pretended to discover the body?

"It might even be one of the townies," Kendra suggested. "Over the years, Mallory's alienated just about every shopkeeper on Main Street. Or maybe someone from Hollywood drove up and bumped her off.

"For all we know," she added, pointing at Cathy, "it was you!"

"Me!" Cathy blinked, stunned. "You're crazy!"

It did seem like a zany idea. Cathy was the one person in this joint who actually seemed to like Mallory. But maybe she figured Mallory's autographed cocktail napkin would be worth more money on eBay if Mallory was dead. A pretty flimsy motive for murder, but it was the best I could come up with.

After Cathy's outburst, we all just sat there in an uneasy silence, waiting to be questioned.

One by one, the others were called in.

Finally it was my turn.

The cop who ushered me into the dining room was a tall good looking dame with pouty lips and a body that wouldn't quit. And her partner was no slouch in the looks department, either. Craggy and tan, he looked like he'd just come from a GQ photo shoot.

For the purposes of this narrative, I'll call them Brad and Angelina.

But their looks were the last thing on my mind when I stepped into the dining room. For the first time since I'd shown up at diet hell, I actually smelled something delicious!

I looked over at the table Brangelina had commandeered for their investigation and saw two humungous, half-eaten deli sandwiches. Hers looked like roast turkey and ham. His, roast beef and swiss. Both had bags of chips and pickles.

"Hope you don't mind if we eat while we do this," Brad said. "We didn't get a chance to have lunch."

Was he kidding? It was all I could do not to hurl myself at their chow and make a run for it.

But somehow I managed to contain myself.

They started with some routine questions about

my name, age and occupation, all of which I answered staring fixedly at their sandies, praying one of them would offer me a bite.

"So did you?" Brad was asking me.

Oh, dear. I'd been so intent on a piece of swiss cheese dangling from his Kaiser roll, I hadn't heard his question.

"Did I what?"

"Hear anything at all during your massage that might give us a clue to the killer's identity?"

"Afraid not."

Unless George Clooney was the killer, I hadn't heard a peep.

"Do you have any idea," Angelina asked between bites of her ham and turkey, "who might have wanted to kill Mallory?"

I hesitated to rat on my fellow guests, but there was a murderer among us. I couldn't just sit by and pretend that Mallory was adored by one and all.

I ran down my list of suspects—just about everyone—and was about to offer them my services as a part-time semiprofessional P.I. (You'd never know it to look at me, but I have solved a few murders in my day, which you can read all about in the titles listed at the front of this book.)

But just then they threw me a most unwelcome curve ball.

"What was *your* relationship with the deceased like?" Angelina asked.

"What relationship?? I barely knew the woman."

"That's not what we heard."

"Huh?"

"According to our notes," Brad said, taking time out from his sandwich to flip through a small pad, "the other night at dinner, you offered Mallory your services as a writer."

I thought back to that first dinner when blabbermouth Cathy, upon hearing that Mallory needed a writer, piped up and suggested *moi*.

"I didn't offer my services. Cathy did."

"Whatever. We have an eyewitness who confirmed that Mallory Francis was quite insulting in her reply to you. Suggesting you weren't a real writer."

Oh, for crying out loud. Who the heck felt the need to share *that* little anecdote?

"So?" I shrugged. "Mallory dissed me. She dissed everybody."

"Writers can be very sensitive," Brad said.

"High strung," Angelina chimed in.

"You think I'd strangle Mallory with a piece of kelp because she said I wasn't a real writer?"

"Stranger things have happened."

"Well, I can assure you, I didn't do it."

"Nevertheless, we'd like you to stick around for a few days. Understood?"

"Understood," I nodded, steamed to the max. The nerve of these people, practically accusing me of murder!

"Any questions?" Brad asked, licking some mustard from his finger.

"Just one," I said.

Brangelina looked up at me inquiringly.

"You guys gonna eat your pickles?"

Chapter 14

I allowed myself the faint hope that Olga might cancel our classes out of respect for the not-so-dearly departed. But alas, that night over celery fizzes, Olga announced that, murder or no murder, it was business as usual at The Haven. Same nine hundred miserable calories a day. Same god-awful exercises.

Whatever uneasiness had descended upon the gang in the aftermath of Mallory's death was gone by dinner. Olga was positively buoyant as she dished out the evening's slop (gray chicken, soggy zucchini, and—alert the media!—cantaloupe instead of mangoes for dessert).

Kendra had taken Mallory's place at the "A" table, and for once, I saw a smile on her face. After a whole thirteen seconds of pretending to mourn her sister's death, she and Harvy and Clint were laughing and telling jokes, in the highest of high spirits. Every once in a while, Olga would join in with a bon mot of her own.

Even Armani, the Peke, seemed to be in a jolly mood, digging into his steak tidbits with gusto.

Here with me at the peasant table, though, Cathy was a nervous wreck, still convinced one of her fellow guests was a killer.

"Not you, of course, "she whispered to me. "I know you didn't do it. But I wouldn't trust those others as far as I could throw a celery stick.

"How I wish I were back in Duluth scanning Pringles at the Piggly Wiggly," she moaned. "I should have listened to Mr. Muffin. He told me not to go away and leave him in the kennel."

She was right, of course. Not about Mr. Muffin. I had no idea whether he was in psychic communication with his mistress.

But I did know that someone at The Haven was a killer. And I was still steaming over Brangelina's insinuation that it might be me. I made up my mind then and there to do a little investigating of my own. The sooner the Spa Strangler was found, the sooner I could go home to my Chunky Monkey-stocked refrigerator.

Back in my room, I saw Prozac out on the patio staring at the koi pond.

You'll be pleased to know that in my absence she finally got a vigorous workout with her Whirlybird exercise toy.

I found the feathered remains of the poor thing scattered everywhere.

"Prozac," I said, plucking a feather from the bowl of flowers on the dresser, "how could you?"

She glared at me, affronted, and began swishing her tail in an Academy Award-winning performance of a Long-Suffering Kitty.

How could I???? Trapped in this diet dungeon with nothing to eat but a measly can of Fancy Feast? No wonder I went after that idiotic Whirlybird. If I don't get something in my tummy soon, there's no telling how long I'll last! At this stage of the game, I'll eat anything, I tell you! Anything!

"Here," I said, holding out the gray chicken I'd smuggled from dinner. "I brought you this."

She took one look at it, and wrinkled her pink nose in disgust.

Eeeeu. I can't eat that.

Is she impossible, or what?

"It'll have to do, until I get back from my food run," I said, plopping it in her bowl.

After gathering poor Mr. Bird's remains and hiding them in my suitcase (heaven knows what punishment Frau Olga would mete out if she discovered them), I headed off to town.

I'd cleverly donned cargo pants and a jacket with plenty of pockets to store the goodies I planned to buy. I intended to dash into Darryl's Deli to load up on calories and a quick peek at the eminently peek-worthy Darryl, then hurry back to feed Prozac, who'd been meowing piteously when I left, draped over the back of the armchair, very Sarah Bernhardt On Her Deathbed.

But you know how it is with best laid plans.

Driving through town, I happened to see that

the pizza parlor was open. Even from my car, I could smell the garlic wafting from the exhaust vent. Mind you, I'd been dreaming of that pizza ever since I'd first seen the restaurant from the top of Mount Olga.

The lure of garlic was too powerful to resist. The next thing I knew, I was pulling into the parking lot.

I'd just run in for a quickie slice to go. I'd be in and out in five minutes. Six, tops.

But once again my plans were derailed. Because the first thing I noticed when I stepped inside, other than the heady aroma of garlic and sausages, was Harvy and Kendra sitting at a table, a pizza and pitcher of beer on the red checkered tablecloth between them.

What a perfect opportunity to start my investigation. Princess Prozac would just have to wait.

I trotted up to Mallory's former posse, a suitably mournful but friendly smile on my face.

"Hi, there. What a surprise running into you two like this."

Kendra looked up from her beer with bloodshot eyes.

"Not really," she replied, slurring her words. "Sooner or later everybody at The Haven winds up here."

Aha. So I wasn't the only inmate who cheated.

"Mind if I join you?" I asked, pulling out a chair before they could say no.

"Sure," Harvy said, with an expansive wave of his beer stein. "Have a seat."

I horned myself in between them and got right down to business.

Okay, I didn't get right down to business. I took one look at their pizza and forgot all about the interview. Gosh, that thing looked good. Sausages and mushrooms, swimming in a sea of thick gooey cheese.

"Help yourself," Harvy said, no doubt noticing the pizza lust in my eyes.

He and Kendra watched in disbelief as I wolfed it down in record time.

"Care for another slice?" Harvy asked.

Before he'd even finished the question, slice number two was in my mouth.

"Miss!" Kendra called out to our waitress. "Another sausage and mushroom pizza. Looks like we're gonna need it."

Then she turned to Harvy and, in a stage whisper that could be heard in Fresno, said, "Better grab a slice while you can."

"Guess I was a little hungry." I smiled apologetically when I'd finished inhaling.

"I'd hate to see her when she's starving," Kendra muttered into her beer.

"I'll be happy to pay you for what I ate."

"No, that's okay," Harvy said, staring at the empty space where the pizza slices had been. "It's our treat."

"Thanks so much."

My feeding frenzy abated, at last I remembered my mission.

"I can't believe I've been sitting here all this time and haven't offered you my condolences about Mallory."

"It hasn't been that long," Harvy said. "I think

you ate that pizza in less than thirty seconds. It could be a world record."

Okay, so I ate fast. He didn't have to make such a big production over it.

"As I was saying," I said, eager to drop the topic of my speed eating. "I want to express my condolences on the untimely demise of your sister, Kendra. It was a real tragedy."

"Yeah," Kendra said, in a voice singularly devoid of sorrow, "a real tragedy." She hoisted her beer stein in a toast. "To my dearly departed sister. Here's hoping they serve mangoes in hell."

Harvy clinked his glass against hers and they wasted no time slugging down their beer.

Something told me it wasn't their first pitcher.

"I just got off the phone with her attorney," Kendra groused, "and would you believe that selfish bitch left me only fifty grand?"

Wow, she sure hadn't wasted any time making *that* phone call.

"She left a hundred grand to the gal who gave her botox shots, for crying out loud! A million for the care and feeding of Armani. And the rest to the Mallory Francis Foundation for Abused Pekes."

She slammed down her beer stein in disgust.

"How many abused Pekes are there on the planet, anyway? Zero, that's how many! Armani will be vacationing at the Ritz Carlton and I'll be stuck with fifty measly grand."

Of course, fifty thousand dollars sounded like a gold mine to me, but obviously Kendra had been expecting more. Much more. And once again, I wondered if she'd bumped off her sister to get it.

Harvy reached over and took her hand, a reasonable facsimile of sympathy in his eyes. "I'd give you some of my money, hon, but I need it for the salon. But you can come in any time for a free cut and color."

"Thanks a ton," Kendra sighed. "At least I'll look good on the unemployment line."

"I wish it could be more, but I've already signed the lease and everything."

"Hey, not to worry. It's not your fault my sister was such a bitch."

"I'll drink to that," Harvy said, guzzling down some more suds. "Remember the time she flew me back from my uncle's funeral to blow out her bangs? And then she expected me to reimburse her for the plane ticket!"

"How awful," I commiserated. Lord knows how many resentments he'd stored away over the years. Probably enough to want to see her dead. Maybe even enough to kill her himself.

"Mallory was always pulling off stunts like that," Kendra said.

"Did she really send out that assistant director to buy mangoes in a hurricane?" I asked.

"Yeah," Kendra nodded. "Poor Pablo. Crashed his car and was injured pretty badly. Heard he wound up in a wheelchair."

"And what about the makeup lady she fired just as her little boy was about to go into the hospital for surgery?" Harvy chimed in, tripping down miserable memory lane.

"Poor thing lost her health insurance," Kendra said. "Did Mallory care? No, she was just annoyed she had to break in a new makeup lady. No wonder somebody killed her. Frankly, I'm surprised it took so long."

"Do you have any idea who might have done it?" I asked.

"Half the population of Hollywood had a motive. But I still think it's that masseuse."

"Me, too," Harvy seconded. "I heard Sven and Mallory going at like bunnies last night. Shawna had to know about it."

"Are you kidding?" Kendra sniffed. "If I know Mallory, she was probably bragging to Shawna about it."

"Besides," Harvy pointed out, "Shawna's the one who was in the room with Mallory, giving her the seaweed wrap."

All very true, of course. Shawna had both motive and opportunity. But I couldn't help wondering why she'd kill Mallory during the seaweed wrap, knowing she'd be the obvious suspect. Why wouldn't she wait for some other chance to strangle her rival in romance?

If you ask me, both Kendra and Harvy had equally strong motives for killing Mallory. Who's to say they weren't pointing fingers at Shawna to throw suspicion off themselves?

For all I knew, the killer was right there at my table, scarfing down a Heineken.

Chapter 15

I left Mallory's former posse bitching into their beers and dashed over to Darryl's, popping an Altoid en route—just in case my deli doll was behind the counter.

Oh, goodie. He was.

"Welcome back!" He grinned as I walked in the door.

"Hi, there," I replied, my heart melting at the sight of his laugh lines.

"How did you and Grammy Austen like the fudge sauce last night?"

"Never got a chance to try it," I sighed. "I got busted at the front door by Olga."

"Oh, I'm so sorry. I should have warned you to be careful. She's got eyes like a hawk."

"I learned my lesson. This time," I said, pointing to my cargo pockets, "I'm prepared to smuggle my loot into my room."

"Smart thinking."

He smiled again.

My heart melted again.

Then, after an awkward second or two during which he did not take me in his arms and cover me with baby kisses, I said, "Guess I'd better get my groceries."

I grabbed a cart and headed down the aisles, praying my tush didn't look too big.

A few minutes later I was back with my loot.

"Find everything you want?" he asked.

"Possibly, now that I've met you."

Of course, I didn't really say that. I just nodded and wowed him with the delightfully witty, "Yes, thanks."

"I hope you're not too upset about what happened at the spa today," he said, as he started bagging my stuff.

"Upset? About what?"

"Mallory Francis's murder."

Oh, for crying out loud. Can you believe I'd forgotten all about it? Shows you what a few laugh lines on the right face can do.

"Right. The murder. What a terrible thing."

"Everybody in town's been talking about it."

"Any idea who did it?" I asked, hoping he'd heard some juicy gossip.

"Not a clue," he shrugged. "Although word on the street is that Olga hated Mallory's guts."

"Just one of many, I'm afraid."

"How's your grandmother taking it?"

I wish he'd stop focusing so much on dear old Grammy Austen.

"Grammy's fine. She's a tough old gal."

"Just be careful," he said, his brow furrowed

in concern. "After all, there's a murderer on the loose."

"Oh, I will," I assured him.

Another awkward moment while I waited in vain for him to take me in his arms and declare undying love and/or momentary lust.

"Well, see ya," I said, starting for the door.

"Wait!" he called out.

I turned to face him.

"Let me make it up to you for getting caught last night," he said. "I should have warned you about Olga standing guard at the front door."

"Oh, that's okay."

"No, really. I owe you one. How about we go grab a bite of dinner?"

"What about the deli? Don't you need to be here?"

"I can close if I want. I'm the boss. So how about it?"

Cat lovers everywhere will be horrified to learn that, at that moment, all thoughts of my hungry kitty waiting impatiently for her chow flew from my brain.

"Dinner sounds great," I said, also ignoring the fact that I'd just packed away two (okay, three) slices of sausage and mushroom pizza. Surely, I could make room in my tummy for some of Darryl's homemade cannelloni.

He got up from behind the counter, and joined me at the door. In jeans and a sweatshirt, he had that lanky Ichabod Crane bod I'm particularly partial to. (Obviously an opposites attract kind of thing.)

"Want to go for pizza?" he asked, slipping into a windbreaker. "I've been craving some all day."

Pizza? Oh, crud. What if Harvy and Kendra were still at the pizza parlor and spilled the beans that I'd just been stuffing my face? The last thing I needed was for Darryl to think I was the kind of gal who went for pizza twice in one night. But what else could I suggest? Le Petit Ripoff? Not bloody likely.

"Um, sure," I said. "Pizza sounds fab."

Darryl locked up the deli, and after putting my groceries in my car, we started walking down Main Street.

I prayed there was another pizza parlor in town, one I hadn't noticed, down a side street, perhaps. But alas, Darryl took me to the place I'd just left not more than twenty minutes ago.

To my immense relief, Harvy and Kendra were gone when we got there.

Darryl led me to a cozy booth for two, and was sitting across from me, smiling that killer smile of his, when I heard:

"You back again?"

Oh, hell. It was the waitress I'd had with Harvy and Kendra, a punk redhead with a most disconcerting diamond stud in her nose.

"Yes," I said with as much dignity as I could muster under the circs. "Back again."

"So what'll it be?" she said, taking out her order pad.

"Is sausage and mushroom okay with you?" Darryl asked.

"Oh, it's fine with her," Ms. Punk piped up. "You want extra mushrooms like the last time?"

"Yes, that would be lovely," I said with a stiff smile.

If only I had some kelp handy; I knew whose neck I'd like to wring.

"You've been here before?" Darryl asked as she skipped off.

"Um, yes. Grammy and I stopped by the other day before we checked into The Haven. Sort of a last hurrah before Grammy started her diet. I guess the waitress remembered me."

"Speaking of your Grammy, are you sure she won't mind your taking time to have dinner like this? Won't she be hungry?"

"Oh, no. She was napping when I left. Grammy loves to nap."

Then, eager to get off the Grammy track, I asked, "So tell me, have you always lived here?"

"No, I just moved here two years ago from L.A. I used to be a stockbroker, but I'm afraid I wasn't cut out for it. Every time my clients lost money, I lost sleep."

Omigosh, a stockbroker with a heart! Was he a sweetie, or what?

"So I cashed out my savings and bought the deli. Got myself a little bungalow up in the hills, and when I'm not working at the deli, I'm trying to write my Great American Novel."

"You're writing a novel? That's wonderful! I've always wanted to do that."

He blushed a most becoming shade of Aw Shucks Pink and asked, "So what about you? What do you do when you're not dieting with your grammy?"

"Actually, I'm a writer, too."

"You are?" His eyes lit up, impressed. "What have you written?"

For the briefest instant, I considered telling him that I dashed off ad campaigns for IBM and Procter & Gamble, but my whopper about Grammy Austen was bad enough, so I decided to stick with the truth.

"I write ads for local L.A. clients. Ackerman's Awnings. Fiedler on the Roof Roofers. Toiletmasters Plumbers."

"Toiletmasters?? You wrote *In a rush to Flush? Call Toiletmasters!*? I used to see that commercial in the middle of the night back in L.A. when I couldn't sleep!"

"Yes, many people have told me it's a highly effective sleep aid."

At which point, Ms. Punk showed up with our wine and pizza.

"Here you go," she said to me. "*Again*."

Where the heck was that kelp when I needed it?

As she trotted off to harass her other customers, Darryl cut me a giant slab of pizza.

I gazed down at it, and guess what, folks? For once in my life, I wasn't ready to swan dive into my plate.

Maybe it was the excitement of being across the table from Darryl; maybe it was the three (okay, four) slices I'd had earlier, but I just wasn't hungry.

"Well, dig in!" Darryl said.

I began picking at my pizza, just like the Size 0 movie stars do in scenes that require them to put food in their mouths, quite enjoying the image of myself as a finicky eater.

The next several minutes passed in a happy
blur as Darryl and I continued chatting, him
telling me about life as a deli owner and aspiring writer, me nodding a lot and trying to figure
out if his eyes were brown or hazel. Before long
I was lost in a daydream of the two of us living
together in his cozy bungalow in the hills, Darryl writing his Great American Novel and me
writing long distance ads for Toiletmasters. Just
as I was picturing the two of us sitting down to a
home-cooked cannelloni dinner, with Ben &
Jerry and dipsy doodle for dessert, I heard:

"Jaine, are you okay?"

I snapped back to reality and saw Darryl looking at my plate. "You've hardly touched your
pizza."

"I'm not all that hungry," I said, in a moment
straight out of *Ripley's Believe it Or Not*.

"Wow. You really eat like a bird."

Oh, Lordy. If he only knew.

Darryl walked me back to his parking lot in
the cool night air, the moon a sliver in the sky
above.

We'd lingered over our pizza, gabbing like
crazy, the usual getting-to-know-you chatter
about favorite books and movies. I was thrilled to
discover that, in addition to P.G. Wodehouse,
we both loved Anne Tyler, *Sunset Boulevard* and
Roman Holiday. And guess what? He didn't like
The Three Stooges! Hated them, in fact.

That alone practically qualified him for saint-
hood.

"I just don't get that whole 'nyuck, nyuck, nyuck' thing," he'd said, shaking his head.

Yes, I'd felt a definite connection over pizza.

But now, as our footsteps echoed in the empty streets, an awkward silence fell between us.

I tried to think of something clever to say when we got back to my car, but all I could come up with was, "Thanks so much for the pizza."

"My pleasure," he replied.

I looked up into his eyes (hazel, definitely hazel), at his shaggy hair grazing the collar of his sweatshirt, and at that fabulous smile, hoping he'd soon be zeroing in for a kiss.

"Well, see ya," he said, making no move whatsoever to lock lips.

Swallowing my disappointment, I got in my Corolla, and was about to put the key in the ignition when he tapped on my window. I rolled it down, and he leaned in toward me.

Okay, this was it, the moment I'd been waiting for—our first big smackeroo.

But no, he just reached in and plucked a slice of mushroom from my sweatshirt.

Oh, damn. Even picking at my food, I'd managed to spill something. I can't take me anywhere.

"Drive safely," he said. "And give my best to Grammy Austen."

"Will do," I assured him with a weak smile, and took off into the night.

And as I drove back to The Haven I proceeded to read myself the riot act.

I really had to stop my ridiculous habit of fantasizing about guys I'd barely met. Here I'd built up this whole romantic Girl Meets Aspiring Writer/Deli Owner fairy tale, complete with Cozy Bungalow-For-Two happy ending, before the poor guy had even finished his first slice of pizza.

Darryl was just a cute guy who got lonely at his deli and wanted some company while he went for pizza. And I just happened to be at the checkout counter when he got the munchies.

No big fairy tale romance. No prince charming. Just a guy in the mood for pizza.

That's it. End of story. *Finito.*

Back at The Haven, I groaned to see Olga at the reception desk, busily making notes in a ledger.

Rats. If only I'd snuck in the back door! What if she realized the bulges in my cargo pocket weren't muscles?

Before I knew it, her eagle eyes were boring into me.

"Where have you been?" she asked, in full-tilt Gestapo mode.

"Out walking," I said.

Which technically was no lie. I had, after all, walked all the way from the deli to the pizza parlor.

"Is that so?" she asked, her voice dripping with skepticism.

She got up and took a step toward me.

Uh-oh. I felt a strip search coming on. But just then the phone rang. Olga stared at it longingly, torn between nabbing a diet scofflaw or a potential customer.

Thank heavens, the customer won.

"Oh, what the hell," she said finally, waving me by to pick up the phone and trill a sugary hello to the caller.

One dragon down, one to go.

Needless to say, Prozac was more than a tad miffed when I got back to our room.

She looked up from where she'd been pacing and shot me a venomous glare.

What the heck took you so long?

"I'm so sorry I'm late, sweetheart. I was busy conducting an important investigation."

She practically rolled her eyes at that one.

Oh, please. I can smell the sausage on your breath from here.

And without any further ado, she began yowling to be fed.

I reached into my cargo pockets, where I'd stashed several cans of Darryl's gourmet cat food—along with a blueberry muffin, a turkey and swiss cheese sandwich, and a couple Almond Joys to get me through the next day.

"Look what Mommy got you, love bug!" I held up a can of cat food in triumph. "Hearty Halibut Entrails!"

Prozac swished her tail impatiently.

How many times do I have to tell you? You're not my mommy. And don't call me love bug! Just open the darn can before I start eating the carpet!

"I'm opening it right now!"

And that's when tragedy struck.

When I looked down at the Hearty Halibut

Entrails, I realized Darryl's gourmet cat food didn't come with a pop top.

And guess who forgot to buy a can opener?

Minutes later, I was frantically prowling the hallway, searching for Delphine. I found her in the supply closet, stocking her cart with M&N's.

"Thank God you're here!" I cried. "I need a can opener ASAP! Please tell me that you've got one!"

"This is your lucky day," she said with a perky nod of her ponytail. "It just so happens I'm running a sale on can openers."

She reached down into her cart and pulled out a rusty relic of a can opener, crusted with ancient food stains.

"How much?"

"For you, thirty bucks."

"Thirty bucks?" I blinked in outrage. "For a used can opener?"

"Better make up your mind. Sale ends soon. Then it goes up to fifty."

"That's highway robbery!" I shrieked.

"So I've been told," she smiled blandly.

I was all set to storm off in a huff and go back to Darryl's, but then I remembered Darryl had closed up shop. Of course it was possible he'd opened again after I left him in the parking lot, but I couldn't risk it. Heaven help me if the deli was closed and I came back without that can opener. Prozac would probably make me open the darn can with my teeth.

"Tick tock, tick tock," Delphine said, pointing at her watch.

"Wait a minute," I sighed. "I'll get my checkbook."

Thirty dollars later, Prozac was burying her little pink nose in a can of Hearty Halibut Entrails.

And I was writing a very nasty e-mail to Lance.

YOU'VE GOT MAIL

To: Jausten
From: DaddyO
Subject: The Great Debate

Fantastic news, Lambchop! I've challenged the battleaxe to a debate! Not only that, it's going to be televised live on Tampa Vistas' closed circuit TV. At long last I'll be able to expose Lydia Pinkus for the petty tyrant she really is.

I don't care what your mom says—*PINKUS STINKS!*

More later,

XXX

Daddy (aka "Mr. President")

To: Jausten
From: Shoptillyoudrop
Subject: On the Warpath

I suppose Daddy's told you about his debate with Lydia. Somehow he managed to talk Artie Myers into televising the debate live on Channel 99, Tampa Vistas' closed circuit TV station. Artie's the fellow in charge of Channel 99 programming. Which is mostly just a list of clubhouse activities and items for sale. But occasionally they do broadcasts. Last year, they shot George and Gloria Martin's 50th wedding anniversary, which turned quite dramatic when the happy couple got into the most horrible fight about George's habit of sucking his teeth which Gloria said had been driving her nuts for the past fifty years. But until Gloria threw that glass of champagne in George's lap, it was really very sweet.

But I'm rambling, aren't I? The fact is Daddy has insisted on debating Lydia, and I'm sure he'll live to regret it. Why, Lydia is one of the most dynamic speakers I know. She'll mop the floor with your father. Oh, well. It'll serve him right for that *PINKUS STINKS* sign!

Right now he's in the garage, making podiums of all things! Artie wanted to shoot the debate with the two candidates sitting at a table. But no, that wasn't good enough for Daddy, who wants to stand behind podiums "just like they do on the real presidential elections."

Oh, dear. All that hammering is giving me a headache.

More later, honey. I need an aspirin.

XXX

Mom

PS. You're not going to believe this, but now Daddy expects me to call him "Mr. President."

To: Jausten
From: DaddyO
Subject: Ta Da!

I finished my podiums, and if I do say so myself, they're works of art!

Now I'm off to take them to the clubhouse. I just hope they fit in my "election-mobile."

XXX

Daddy (aka "Mr. President")

To: Jausten
From: Shoptillyoudrop
Subject: Cardboard Coffins

You should see the rickety boxes Daddy is calling podiums. He's carting them over to the clubhouse right now. They're sticking out from the trunk of his Camry like two cardboard coffins.

Oh, well. At least the hammering has stopped. Now I can concentrate on the Aztec & Incan history book Professor Rothman assigned us to read. Would you believe that the Aztecs invented both mandatory education *and* chewing gum! Imagine those poor Aztec janitors. Having to clean the first gum from the desks of the first kids forced to go to school!

Isn't history just fascinating?

Love & kisses from,

Mom

To: Jausten
From: Sir Lancelot
Subject: How Exciting!

Sweetie, I just heard about Mallory's murder. How exciting! And to think, you would have missed it all if it hadn't been for me!

Crazy busy at work. Thank heavens I got a chance to unwind at dinner. Went to the most wonderful burrito joint in Culver City. The chimichangas were magnifico!

Hug hug, kiss kiss,

Lance

Chapter 16

"I didn't sleep a wink last night," Cathy said as we struggled up Mt. Olga on our nature hike the next morning, lagging behind the others as usual.

I hadn't had the most peaceful night myself, having once again read my parents' e-mails right before going to sleep. The thought of Daddy debating Lydia Pinkus on live TV kept my worry genes bubbling for quite a while.

The last time Daddy was on camera was at my cousin Joanie's wedding, when the videographer caught him eating one of the frosted flowers off the wedding cake before it had even been cut. The footage of him being escorted out by the security guards was particularly riveting.

Heaven knows what would happen when he hit the stage with Lydia.

"Honestly, Jaine," Cathy was saying, yanking

me out of my reverie, "I was so scared, I kept a can of mace under my pillow all night. What if someone is out to get me?"

"Why on earth would anyone be out to get you?"

Other than to put an end to her incessant yapping, I couldn't think of a single reason.

"Because," she replied, lowering her voice to an excited whisper, "I think I may have seen the killer."

Hallelujah! A lead! With any luck, thanks to Chatty Cathy, we could all be going home by the end of the day.

"You actually saw someone going into Mallory's spa cubicle?"

"No. It was earlier in the day. I'd just finished working in the organic garden. Frankly, I'm beginning to think Olga's got a lot of nerve putting us to work like that. You should see the back of my neck. I forgot to put on sunblock and it's red as a beet. Look."

She turned to show me her red neck.

Was the woman impossible, or what? Here she was babbling about her sunburn when she'd possibly seen the Spa Strangler.

I tamped down my impatience and managed to summon a sympathetic *tsk* for her sunburn.

"Getting back to the killer . . . ?" I prompted.

"Oh, right. I was coming in the back door from the garden when I saw someone hurrying down the hallway from the kitchen. At the time I didn't think anything of it, but now I'm beginning to wonder if the person I saw had been stealing some of Olga's valium to drug our tea."

"So who was it?" I said, eager to wrap up this case and be on my way to the nearest McDonald's.

"That's just the problem," she sighed. "It was so bright outside and I'd forgotten my sunglasses along with my sunblock. So when I stepped inside, it took my eyes a while to adjust to the dim corridor."

"You couldn't tell if it was a man or a woman?"

"It may have been a man, but I can't be sure. It might've been a woman, too."

"Do you remember what this person was wearing?"

"Not really. It could have been shorts. Or maybe a jog suit."

Good heavens. Cancel that Quarter Pounder. Helen Keller would make a better eyewitness than Cathy.

By now we'd reached the top of Mt. Olga.

"It's about time!" Olga clucked when she saw us.

The others, who were sitting on the ground taking a breather, looked up at us with thinly veiled impatience. Kendra had wasted no time in raiding her sister's closet and was decked out in one of Mallory's designer jog suits. How she and Harvy had managed to trot up Mt. Olga after their beer toot last night was beyond me.

"Okay, everybody." Olga gave a shrill blast of her whistle. "Rest period is over."

"But Cathy and I just got here," I protested.

"That's not my fault. Now it's time to go back."

Another blast of her whistle, and she was

marching downhill, the "A" listers hot on her heels.

"She can blow her dratted whistle all she wants," I muttered. "I'm not going back down till I catch my breath."

"Well, I'm not going without you," Cathy said, hovering at my side.

We stood in silence for the next minute or so, looking out at the ocean, when suddenly we heard a rustling in the woods behind us.

"Omigod!" Cathy whispered, clutching my arm. "It's the killer come to get me!"

"Don't be silly," I said, "It's probably just an animal." I took her by the elbow. "Let's go back down."

"I can't," she said, frozen to the spot. "What if it's the killer and he springs out from the trees and attacks me like Norman Bates in *Psycho?*"

If she kept this up, we'd be here until dinner.

"Look, I'll go scout out the path and make sure nobody's there, okay?"

"Okay." She nodded doubtfully.

I started down the path, cursing Cathy for being such a drama queen, when I heard the sound of footsteps stomping through the brush. Now it was my turn to be scared. I told myself it was just some forest critter, that I was being utterly ridiculous, when someone came lurching out onto the path.

Not a forest critter—but a man, holding an axe!

Yikes. Cathy was right! It *was* just like Norman Bates in *Psycho!*

"Oh, hi, Ms. Austen."

I blinked and realized it was Kevin, the teen-age chef, now swinging the axe in a wide arc.

Omigosh! Was it possible? Was Kevin some sort of teen serial killer?

I could see the headlines now:

WOULD-BE APPLEBEE'S CHEF SECRET
HOMICIDAL MANIAC!

"Kevin," I gulped, "what are you doing here?"

"Olga sent me to pick mushrooms for lunch."

"With an axe?"

"I'm supposed to get kindling wood for the fireplace, too."

For the first time I noticed he was carrying a muslin sack in his other hand.

"Look," he said, opening the sack, which I saw was stuffed with mushrooms. "They grow like wildfire here."

He bent down to pick another from the ground.

"Although I keep forgetting which ones are poisonous. Don't worry, though. Olga almost always knows the difference."

"How comforting."

"Well, see you later, Ms. Austen. Gotta get the kindling wood."

As he waved good-bye and disappeared into the woods, I made my way back up to Cathy.

"Thank God you're still alive!" she cried when she saw me. "What happened?"

"It was just Kevin, picking mushrooms and getting kindling wood."

"How do you know he didn't just say that? How do you know he's not the killer?"

"Because if he were the killer, we'd be dead by now."

"You've got a point," she conceded.

"Try not to worry, Cathy. I'm sure everything's going to be okay. Maybe whoever you saw running out of the kitchen wasn't even the killer."

"You think?" she asked, a ray of hope in her eyes.

"Of course!" I fibbed, not at all certain Cathy hadn't witnessed the Spa Strangler on the run.

If only the impossible woman had worn her sunglasses!

When at last we'd staggered down from Mt. Olga, Cathy told the Diet Nazi she had a migraine and asked to be excused from the rest of the morning's activities.

Amazingly, Olga gave her permission, and I filed away that handy dandy migraine excuse for future reference.

"Do you really have a headache?" I asked Cathy before she started back to her room.

"Nah. I just want to keep my distance from the killer. I'm going to lock myself in my room, and I don't intend to answer the door for anyone. Not even that awful maid. Do you know she tried to sell me a Snickers bar for twenty-five dollars?"

"Wow. I didn't know Delphine sold Snickers."

"You're not thinking of buying one, are you?" she asked, suddenly remembering her self-appointed role as my diet buddy.

"Of course not," I lied.

She shot me a dubious look.

"Well, see you later," I said, eager to avoid a diet lecture. "And try not to worry."

"I'll be okay," she assured me with what I sensed was a bit of false bravado. "I've got my mace—and an exercise bar I stole from the gym.

"But if I'm not down for lunch," she added, "call the police."

Chapter 17

Cathy wasn't the only no-show in aerobics class. Harvy came trotting into the gym a good twenty minutes late.

"Sorry," he said to Sven, "I had an errand to run."

Depositing a check at the bank, no doubt.

Once again I marveled at how perky he was after all the beer he'd knocked back at the pizza parlor. I guess one hundred grand in the bank will do that to a guy.

He hurried over to join Kendra, breathless with gossip.

"Guess what, Ken? I picked up a copy of the *Times* while I was in town, and Mallory's obit was buried all the way back on page eighteen!"

Kendra's eyes lit up with glee.

"Mallory would be so ticked off!"

"And they used a picture from before her nose job!"

"How delicious!"

Kendra had changed from one of Mallory's jog suits into one of Mallory's body-revealing workout ensembles. And I was amazed to see she had quite a hot bod to reveal. I'd never noticed it before, hidden under the baggy clothes she'd worn. Without Mallory around for unflattering comparisons, Kendra was really rather pretty.

Sven, I saw, was eyeing her with newfound interest.

Good heavens. With Mallory dead less than twenty-four hours, was he already poised to make a new conquest?

Poor Shawna. I sure didn't envy her that marriage.

Shawna wandered among us now, giving half-hearted pointers, a haunted look in her eyes.

Was she still reeling from the trauma of having discovered Mallory's body? Or from the trauma of having killed her?

True, it would have been foolish of Shawna to kill Mallory during the seaweed wrap, when she'd be the most obvious suspect. But maybe she'd acted on impulse in a moment of rage. Maybe Mallory had been bragging about her affair with Sven, and Shawna had snapped, strangling the life out of the woman who was out to steal her man.

I needed to get her alone to question her. But when the class was over, she hurried away before I could stop her. So I lingered behind to talk to Sven.

"What a tragedy about Mallory, huh?" I said, as he gathered up our exercise bars.

"Indeed," he nodded solemnly. "She was a wonderful woman, and a fine Golden Globe-winning actress."

He dropped the exercise bars in their container and turned to me, clearly waiting for me to make my exit.

"I guess we're done," he said, "unless you want to get another body fat measurement."

He pointed to the god-awful Fat Vat in the corner.

"Thanks," I shuddered, "but I think I'll let my fat stay unmeasured for the time being."

"Then if you'll excuse me," he said, all brisk and businesslike, "I've got some work to do."

He started for the small office at the side of the gym.

Not so fast, buster.

"I know you were boffing Mallory," I called out.

He stopped in his tracks, as I knew he would, and whirled around to face me.

"I have no idea what you're talking about."

"Come off it, Sven. I saw you going into Mallory's suite wearing nothing but a smile and a Speedo."

Okay, so I hadn't actually seen him going into her suite, but he didn't know that.

He paled under his perfect tan.

"Would you believe I went there to give her a therapeutic massage?"

"No, I would not."

"Okay," he shrugged, "so we were fooling around. Is that a crime?"

"Sort of, if you're married, and especially, if you're the killer."

"Why on earth would I want to kill Mallory?"

"Maybe you fell madly in love with her and wanted to spend the rest of your life with her. Maybe she laughed at you and told you to take a hike, and you got angry enough to wring the life out of her with a piece of kelp."

"That's ridiculous! I had every reason to keep Mallory alive. She promised she'd get me in the movies."

"And you believed her?"

"Sure, I believed her. She was crazy about me. Most women are."

Wow. If those two had hooked up, they would've needed walk-in closets for their egos.

"I hate to disappoint you, sweetheart," he said, with what was meant to be a beguiling grin, "but I'm not the killer."

"Maybe. Maybe not. But there's a rumor going around The Haven that Shawna is."

Okay, so once again, I exaggerated just a tad.

"That's not true!" For the first time, I saw fear flicker in his eyes. "Shawna couldn't have strangled Mallory. After she settled everybody in their seaweed wraps, she was here with me in the gym the entire time."

"What was she doing in the gym?"

"Yelling at me. She'd found out about me and Mallory and was raking me over the coals like she always does before she forgives me and takes me back."

"She forgave you? Already?" I figured she'd banish him to the sofa for at least a couple of weeks.

"Like I told you. She always does."

Talk about your poster couple for *Cheating Bastards and the Women Who Love Them.*

"Look," he said, "I feel terrible about hurting Shawna, but I couldn't help myself."

At least he had the good grace to look ashamed.

"I know my wife, and I know she's not capable of killing anyone. I swear she was with me the entire time the guests were soaking in seaweed."

Not necessarily the entire time. Shawna could have easily taken a minute or two to strangle her rival in romance. I remembered the look of fury in her eyes when she'd seen Mallory locking lips with her husband.

For all I knew, Sven was lying through his teeth to save his wife's well-toned fanny.

Harvy and I were on Pruning Patrol, hacking away at some hibiscus bushes, the hot sun blazing merrily on our backs.

I, of course, was a virtual Niagara Falls of sweat. But Harvy, in cutoffs and a spanking white sleeveless tank, was enviably moisture-free.

"I never sweat," he boasted. "It's something in my genes."

"Lucky you," I said, wiping a bucket of the stuff from my brow.

He lifted his designer glasses to peer at me.

"Sweetie, do you know what you need?"

"A Mochaccino Smoothie with extra whipped cream."

"Heaven forbid. One more calorie and your hips will have their own zip code."

Well, harty har har. Someone had just promoted himself to Person I'd Like Most to See Behind Bars.

"No, doll," he said. "What you need is a good conditioner and a decent hair cut."

And without even asking my permission, he pulled out the scrunchy from my mop of curls and let my hair fall to my shoulders.

"Omigod. It's worse than I thought. What are you cutting your hair with? A chainsaw?"

Of all the nerve! I happen to pay perfectly good money for my Supercuts.

Definitely time to change the subject and do a little Suspect Grilling.

"Have any luck in the kitchen yesterday?" I asked, as casual as could be.

Once again, he lifted his glasses and peered at me, this time with more than a hint of suspicion in his eyes.

"What on earth are you talking about?"

"Cathy said she thought she saw you hurrying down the hallway from the kitchen."

A tiny fib, but all in the interests of justice.

"I was nowhere near that kitchen," he snapped. "And nowhere near Olga's Valium, if that's what you're implying."

"Gosh, no!" I replied, very babe in the woods. "I thought maybe you were raiding the fridge."

"Yeah, sure," he said, whacking a hibiscus branch with a vengeance. Then he glared at me, suddenly very Perry Mason. "Hey, how do I know *you* didn't take that Valium and put it in our tea? How do I know *you're* not the killer?"

"Me? Why would I want to kill Mallory?"

"She insulted you in public, didn't she? Said you weren't a real writer."

"So you're the one who told that story to the cops!"

"I may have mentioned it in passing," he sniffed.

Nope, I sure wouldn't have minded seeing him behind bars right then.

"Plenty of writers have wanted to kill Mallory. The screenwriter on *Revenge of the Lust Busters* once came after her with a machete. Of course, it was a prop machete, made of rubber, so she wasn't hurt. Much to everyone's regret. But you writers are all nuts. So for all I know, it was you."

"Well, it wasn't."

We clipped in silence for the next minute or so, before I added, "Although I have to admit, I can't get Mallory's murder out of my mind."

"Is that so?"

"It's strange. Right before I drifted off to sleep during my seaweed wrap, I thought I heard a man's voice in Mallory's cubicle.

Another fib, which, as you've no doubt noticed, happens to be a specialty of mine. But I needed to provoke the guy.

And it worked.

"Are you accusing me of murder?

He turned to face me, his knuckles popping as he clutched his gardening shears.

"Not at all!" I fumphered, suddenly uncomfortable at the thought of being within hacking distance of those shears. "It was probably just a crazy dream. I have them all the time. I once dreamed I was arm wrestling with the Pope."

"I can assure you," he said, not the least bit interested in my sleep history, "I didn't kill Mallory. I may have hated the Mad Cow, but I didn't strangle her. If you heard a man in her room, it was probably Clint Masters."

"Clint?" I asked, as if I hadn't seriously considered that possibility myself.

"I've done his hair and seen his dressing room. The man's got enough Klonopin to put all of Malibu in a coma. It would have been a piece a cake for him to drug our tea."

I often find that in these situations, the less you say, the more your suspects talk. So I just went on clipping the hibiscus.

"You don't really think Clint was in his room, napping, do you?" Harvy went on, as I'd hoped he would. "I, for one, think it's awfully suspicious that he's the only guest who didn't show up for the seaweed wrap. Mallory had some hot dirt on him that she was going to use in her memoirs. She said it would destroy him. He could've been lurking in the Spa Therapy Center men's room, just waiting for the chance to strike. He wouldn't have been the first movie star to kill for his career."

Or the first hairdresser, either.

Chapter 18

Cathy never showed up for lunch.

And although it was lovely to enjoy a chatter-free meal for a change, I was worried about my missing tablemate.

Had she indeed seen the killer racing from the kitchen with a fistful of Olga's Valium? More important, had the killer seen her and decided to get rid of her?

I slogged through lunch impatiently, barely touching my motley plate of mushrooms and arugula tossed in Pine-Sol Vinaigrette. As soon as Olga cleared away our dishes, I passed on dessert (three slivers of kiwi—no great loss) and set out to find Cathy's room.

Wasting no time, I ran around knocking on doors, praying she'd be alive behind one of them.

At last I found her room upstairs at the end of the hallway.

"Who is it?" she replied to my knock.

I sighed with relief at the sound of her voice.

"It's me, Jaine."

Seconds later, I heard her padding across the floor. Then her shadow darkened the peephole and she opened the door a cautious few inches, clad in a pair of cat-covered pajamas. In the background, I heard her TV playing.

"Are you okay?" I asked.

"Sure, I'm fine. I was just watching *I Love Lucy*. The one where Lucy goes on a diet. I can so relate to the pain she feels when she's eating a celery stick and Ethel and Ricky and Fred are eating steaks. But she sticks to her diet. Really, it's such an inspirational episode. I'm so sorry you missed it, Jaine. You could really learn a lot from it."

Okay, alert the media. I'd found the one woman walking the planet who didn't realize that *I Love Lucy* was a comedy.

I felt like a fool for having been so worried about her.

"Aren't you hungry?" I wanted to know.

"I'm fine," she assured me. "Olga sent Delphine up with some chicken noodle soup."

"Campbell's?" I asked, yearning for a bowl of the noodle-studded stuff.

"And some tea and toast," she nodded. "Needless to say, I didn't open the door for Delphine. I made her leave my tray outside. I'm not taking any chances around here."

"You got toast?" I asked, zeroing in on the crucial part of her narrative. "Actual bread? With butter?"

"Yep."

"And jam?"

"Strawberry," she nodded. "Not that I ate the jam, I was feeling too guilty about the calories from the bread and butter."

"Well, if you're not going to eat it, can I have it?"

"No, you can't have it." She tsked in disapproval. "Honestly, Jaine. Murder or no murder, we're here to lose weight.

"And speaking of the murder," she beamed, "I think I may have figured out who did it!"

"Who?"

"I'll tell you at dinner. I'm still working out the details—Oops," she said, checking her watch. "Can't talk now. *Sleepless in Seattle* is about to start."

In the background I could hear the music for the movie's opening credits.

"See you later," she said, shutting the door in my face.

I stood there, shaking my head in disbelief.

The woman was maddening, n'est-ce pas? Here she thought she knew who the killer was, and she was taking time out to watch Tom Hanks make goo goo eyes at Meg Ryan!

I headed back downstairs, ticked off at her for not giving me that jam.

But who cared? Lest you forget, I had one of Darryl's heavenly turkey and swiss cheese sandwiches waiting for me back in my room.

I whizzed down the steps, eager to sink my teeth into Darryl's dense focaccia bread, studded with onion slivers and poppy seeds. But then I had a frightening thought: What if Prozac had beaten me to it?

True, I'd taken the precaution of leaving her some of the turkey from my sandwich for a mid-morning snack. But what if she'd smelled the rest of the sandwich and decided she wanted more? What if she broke into the suitcase where I'd hidden it?

Don't laugh. That cat has been known to open pizza boxes, Chinese takeout cartons, and buckets of extra crispy KFC. Pulling open the zipper on a suitcase would be child's play for my feline food felon.

By now my head was filled with images of Prozac sprawled out on my bed, surrounded by a few focaccia crusts, belching her little heart out. I raced down the corridor to my room, where I fumbled with my key and shoved the door open.

You'll be happy to know that Prozac had not discovered my turkey and swiss treasure.

But, alas, someone else had.

There, sitting in my armchair, my sandwich in her lap, was Olga.

And that's not all she'd dug up.

Displayed on my bed was the rest of my smuggled booty—Prozac's gourmet cat food, my emergency Almond Joys, and a snack bag or three of Doritos.

Not to mention the pathetic remains of poor Mr. Whirly Bird.

Olga arose from the armchair like Zeus popping up on Mount Olympus. Eyes narrowed in disgust, she waved the sandwich in my face.

"What, may I ask, is this?" Without waiting for a reply, she gestured to the swag on my bed. "And all this?"

Prozac, who had been weaving among the cans of cat food under the delusion she was about to be fed, let out an irritated meow.

It's my lunch, lady, and I'd like it now!

Ignoring Prozac's yowls of complaint, Olga turned her eagle eye on yours truly.

"Have you got anything to say for yourself?"

"I sure do! You've got a lot of nerve breaking into my personal property! In certain circles," I didn't hesitate to point out, "that's considered illegal!"

You don't want to mess with us Austens when we get our dander up. And my dander at that moment was ready to bust the dander-o-meter.

Strangely, Olga didn't seem at all fazed.

"I'm perfectly entitled to search through your things," she replied with a smug smile. "It says so right there."

She pointed to the laminated card on the back of the door, the one with the room rates and fire exit instructions. I perused its contents and sure enough there was some ridiculous clause claiming that if the management suspected a patron was sneaking food onto the premises, said management retained the right to conduct an on-site inspection and confiscate said food.

"I'm well within my rights," Olga smirked. "So you can forget about any lawsuit."

And with that, she tossed my sandwich into a Haven plastic laundry bag.

Ten to one she'd be eating it for her dinner.

When she started tossing in the cat food, Prozac's eyes widened in alarm.

Hey, whaddaya think you're doing?

Olga continued dumping stuff in the bag, ignoring Prozac's decibel-shattering wails.

Finally she got to the remains of Mr. W. Bird and happily informed me, "You'll be charged an extra thirty dollars to replace this."

"Oh, please. That thing couldn't have cost more than a buck ninety-nine."

Prozac eyed the last of Mr. Bird's feathers.

And it needed ketchup, too.

Having gathered all my goodies in her bag, Olga started for the door. But Prozac was having none of this. With an outraged meow, she leaped off the bed and hurled herself at Olga's ankles, clawing at her socks.

Stop, thief!! I'm making a citizen's arrest!

Barely batting an eyelash, Olga grabbed Prozac by the scruff of her neck and dumped her in my arms.

"This," she said, tsking in disapproval, "is the most poorly disciplined cat I've ever met."

Prozac responded with the kind of hiss she usually saves for the vet.

You're no bargain yourself, lady.

As Olga marched out the door, Prozac wriggled free from my grasp and ran out into the hall, yowling all the way.

I'm going to report you to the ASPCA, the ACLU, and Morris the Cat!

I quickly snatched her back into the room, where she began chewing the scenery for all it was worth, now whimpering like Camille on her deathbed.

What're we going to do? I've already gone two hours without a snack! Just look at me! I'm practically skin and bones.

"Calm down, will you? I've got everything under control."

And indeed I did.

We Austens know how to use our noodles in tough times. My strategic planning skills, honed on years of crossword puzzles and living with Prozac, had stood me in good stead.

Figuring that Olga just might be sneaky enough to go nosing around in my room for forbidden calories, I'd taken the rather brilliant precaution of hiding some emergency provisions in my car.

And without any further ado, I headed for the parking lot.

Chapter 19

Free at last from Olga's scrutiny, I sat crouched in my Corolla, wolfing down a somewhat stale blueberry muffin. My taste buds were not exactly thrilled, having been primed for a turkey and swiss, but it was better than nothing.

I'd just licked the crumbs from my fingers and was reaching into the trunk for my emergency can of cat food when I saw a sheriff's cruiser pulling into the lot.

Hallelujah! The cops were back. With any luck, they'd cracked the case and I could go home!

Shoving the cat food in my pants pocket, I trotted over to get the skinny.

Brangelina were sitting in the cruiser in their starched uniforms and reflective sunglasses, the heady aroma of recently eaten burgers and fries wafting from the window.

Fighting back the impulse to ask if there were any leftovers, I greeted them with a cheery smile.

"You guys here to make an arrest?" I asked, hoping they were and that it wasn't me.

"Not yet," Angelina said, as she and Brad got out of the car.

"I hope you don't still consider me a suspect, haha."

I could see my sickly smile bouncing back at me from their sunglasses.

"We'll let you know when you're off the list," Angelina said.

Ouch. Time for a little self-promotion.

"You should know that I happen to be a model citizen. Ex-Brownie, former member of my high school civics club, and a certified State Farm Good Driver for the past seven years."

"We'll keep that in mind," Brad said.

Desperate to score some points, I followed them as they walked toward The Haven, babbling about how Cathy had seen someone running from the kitchen on the day of the murder and how I suspected it was the killer stealing Olga's Valium to drug our tea.

Eagerly I waited for their reaction to this late-breaking bulletin.

But their faces remained stony behind their Ray-Bans.

Probably wondering what to order for dinner.

"Just don't leave town," Brad warned me, as the two of them disappeared inside The Haven.

Curious to see what they were up to, I hurried to the front door and peeked in the lobby, where I saw them talking to Olga at the reception desk.

"We're just going out back to get another sample," I heard Brad say.

Another sample? Of what? Fingerprints, perhaps?

Figuring they had to be going to the scene of the crime, I decided to follow them.

But no way was I going through the lobby. The last thing I wanted was to run into Der Fuhrer and get frisked for hidden cat food.

Instead I scooted around the side of the house. And sure enough, when I got out back, I saw Brangelina making their way over to the Spa Therapy Center. I followed at what I hoped was a safe distance, straining to catch snippets of their conversation.

But all I heard were the words *Jumbo Jack* and *extra cheese.*

See? I told you. They were talking about what to order for dinner!

When they got to the massage center, they did not go inside, but instead walked around to the side of the building.

I sprinted behind a nearby yucca bush, feeling very proud of myself for being such a good shadow. They had absolutely no idea I was on to them.

Crouched down, trying to avoid the yucca's prickly spines, I watched as they snapped on rubber gloves and started scooping dirt into a plastic container.

Why the heck were they taking dirt from The Spa Therapy Center?

I sat there, ears attuned for gems of info, but they spent what seemed like eternities debating the pros and cons of toasting burger buns.

"Toasting it keeps the bun from getting all soggy," Brad said.

"But untoasted keeps it nice and soft," Angelina insisted.

"I'm telling you, toasted's better."

"Is not."

"Is too."

"Is not."

"Is too."

Finally, when I was *thisclose* to impaling them with a yucca leaf, Brad looked down at the dirt and said, "I just hope there's some traces of the tea left."

"Yeah," said Angelina, "I can't believe the lab screwed up the first sample."

And then I realized why they were there. They must've found a wet spot outside one of the windows after the murder and figured the killer had dumped the sedative-laced tea outside. Now they were testing the dirt for traces of the tea.

So whose window was it?

Brangelina were crouched under the third window from the front of the building.

I thought back to how we were lined up for our seaweed wraps. Here on this side of the building, I was first, then Mallory, and then, in the third cubicle—Kendra.

Omigosh. Did that mean Kendra was the killer?

"Although who knows if that wet spot we

found was even tea," Brad sighed. "For all we know it was just water from the sprinkler head."

So much for Kendra's imminent arrest. But if the lab results showed tea under her window, it sure didn't look good for her.

By now Brangelina had packed up their things and were starting back up the path to The Haven.

I held my breath as they walked past me. And as I did I heard Brad say, "Watch out for those yucca spines, Jaine. They can be awfully prickly."

Remind me not to give up my day job.

There was a decided nip in the air when I stepped into my spa cubicle. Shawna, my former angel of mercy, had a gimlet look in her baby blues that did not bode well. She handed me my tea in an icy silence, then marched over to the supply table where she started clattering among the bottles of massage oils.

"So how's it going?" I asked, eager to get the conversational ball bouncing.

"Just dandy," she snapped.

Before I'd barely had a chance to taste my tea, she snatched it away and pointed to the massage table.

"Hop on," she commanded, with nary a trace of a smile.

Once I was settled on the table, a towel tossed carelessly across my privates, she slapped on some exfoliating gloves and began sawing away at my limbs like a 2x4 at a lumber yard. Gone was her gentle touch. The woman had morphed overnight from Florence Nightingale to Dr. Mengele.

When she'd finished mauling my epidermis, she tossed aside her exfoliating gloves and began rubbing me down with massage oil. Last time she'd heated it. Now it was ice cold.

My ministering angel was miffed, all right. And I was about to find out why.

"Sven told me you two had a little chat," she said, rubbing the clammy oil onto my thighs with what I considered a tad too much vigor.

"Oh, that," I said, with a nervous laugh. "It was nothing, really."

"Nothing? You practically accused us both of murder!"

"No! Not at all," I assured her. "I was just asking a few questions."

"What are you, some kind of detective?"

I figured it was best to come clean.

"Part-time, semi-professional," I confessed.

"No way, thunderthighs!"

Okay, so what she really said was, "You sure don't look like one.

"You told Sven," she then reminded me, "that everybody thinks I killed Mallory."

Oh, damn. Why the heck had I made up that idiotic fib?

"Not everybody," I backpedalled. "One or two people may have bandied that theory about, but I'm sure they didn't mean it."

She whipped off the cucumber slices she'd slapped on my eyes, and glared down at me.

"I don't care what anybody says. I didn't kill Mallory. After I got everyone settled in their seaweed wraps, I went to the gym to have it out with Sven. I was gone at least twenty minutes. Anyone could've slipped into Mallory's cubicle during that time."

"Absolutely," I assured her.

"I simply can't believe people would think I'm the killer," she huffed, kneading my arms like Julia Child hacking at a wad of sourdough.

"Mallory *was* making a play for your husband," I pointed out as tactfully as I could. "It's not hard to see why people might think you'd feel threatened."

Another icy glare.

"I didn't need to kill Mallory. I know what kind of man I'm married to. Sven has cheated before. And he'll cheat again. But in the end, he always comes back to me."

She lifted her chin defiantly, but behind that confidence I detected a flicker of unease. Maybe Sven had always come back to her before. But Mallory wasn't your ordinary middle-aged spa guest hoping to drop a few pounds. She was a knockout, a stunner, and a movie star, to boot. I wasn't so sure Sven would have been able to resist her. And neither, I sensed, was Shawna.

"So," she said, as she flipped me over on my stomach and began pummeling my back, "which one or two people told you they thought I killed Mallory?"

"I'm really not at liberty to say. . . . Ouch!"

Good heavens, I'd had mammograms that were less painful than this.

"Just working out the knots," Shawna snapped. "Now I repeat, which one or two people?"

I suddenly realized that my neck was just inches away from those very strong hands.

Best not to get her any angrier than she already was.

"Kendra and Harvy," I admitted.

"Harvy???" Shawna snorted in disdain. "That little twerp? *He's* probably the killer! Now I'm sorry I didn't report him to the cops."

Suddenly I forgot my pummeled muscles and perked up, interested.

"What makes you think Harvy might be the killer?"

"Because when I went to his cubicle to give him his seaweed wrap, he wasn't there. He came hurrying in a few seconds later, said he'd gone to his room to get an aspirin. But why would he do that when he could've just asked me for one? I keep them right here in the supply cabinet. Who's to say he wasn't across the hall strangling Mallory?"

Good question.

Let's all give that some thought between chapters, shall we?

Chapter 20

I left Shawna feeling like I'd just done ten rounds with Evander Holyfield and headed over to the jacuzzi to seek relief for my aching muscles.

Approaching the pool area, I saw Harvy and Kendra stretched out on chaises, Armani dozing on a chaise of his own next to Kendra, a hot pink sun visor perched on his pointy ears.

Harvy and Kendra were leafing through some magazines, and if my eyes did not deceive me, munching on what looked like pretzels. Out in the open, in broad daylight!

For heaven's sake. Was I the only one in this joint who got caught cheating on her diet?

Quickly, I trotted to their side.

Indeed, they were eating pretzels from a bag on a small table between them. The short, thick, stubby kind, which happen to be my favorite.

"Hi, there!" I said, hoping they'd offer me one.

"Well, well," Harvy sneered. "If it isn't Nancy Drew. Come to arrest me?"

Kendra, decked out in what was probably one of Mallory's bikinis, took time out from the *Vogue* she was reading to shoot me a matching sneer.

"Look, Harvy," I said, eager to make amends, "I'm sorry if I insulted you earlier."

"You should be," he huffed, still pissy.

"I don't really suspect you of murder."

Which was a baldfaced lie, of course. After what Shawna had just told me, he was practically my number one suspect. And Kendra wasn't far behind, what with Brangelina digging for sedative-laced tea outside her cubicle window.

But I needed to say something to put an end to the hostilities and nab myself one of those pretzels.

"Honest, I don't suspect you of anything."

"Oh, fab." Harvy wiped his brow with exaggerated relief. "Now I can sleep easy."

I decided to take the high road and ignore his sarcasm. Instead, I just stood there, eyeing the pretzels, hoping they'd take the hint.

I hoped in vain.

"Anything else you'd care to say?" Harvy asked, clearly waiting for me to make myself scarce.

"I don't suppose you could spare a pretzel?" I finally broke down and asked.

"No," he said, biting into one. "We can't."

Wow. Some people sure know how to hold a grudge.

"I can spare a piece of advice, though," Kendra said, looking up at me through Mallory's designer sunglasses. "You really should be careful, Jaine. If there's a killer among us, chances are, he—or she—won't hesitate to kill again."

Was that a piece of advice I'd just heard—or a threat?

Your guess is as good as mine.

"Well," Kendra said, dismissing me with a cool smile, "see you at cocktail hour."

Then, just as I was about to walk away, Kendra put down her *Vogue* and reached for some sunblock. I blinked in surprise. And not at the Swarovski crystals embedded in her dead sister's bikini top. But rather, at a long gash of a scratch on her chest.

"What happened to your chest?" I asked.

"That damn Armani." The dog's ears perked up at the sound of his name. "I wasn't fast enough feeding Mr. Cranky his doggie treat."

As if to prove his crankiness, Armani bared his tiny teeth and growled.

"And to think," Kendra said, rolling her eyes, "the little monster is going to inherit a million dollars."

I guess I must have still been staring at her scab, because Kendra shot me a glare even more hostile than the one she'd been lobbing at Armani.

"I didn't get it strangling Mallory, if that's what you're wondering."

But of course, that's exactly what I was wondering.

* * *

Okay, class. Let's pause to consider. Did Kendra really get that scratch from Armani? Or had she been clawed by Mallory, fighting for her life on the massage table? And had Harvy really zipped off to his room, as claimed, for an aspirin? Or had he been the one wringing that kelp around Mallory's neck? And what about Shawna, the welterweight masseuse? Had she made a murderous pit stop at Mallory's cubicle between seaweed wraps?

I was soaking my aching muscles in the jacuzzi, pondering these questions and wishing I'd been able to nab a pretzel or two, when I gazed up and saw Clint Masters approaching.

"Hey, there!" he said, throwing off his spa robe and tossing it on a nearby chaise.

Crammed as he was into a tight red Speedo, just about every one of his jumbo muscles were on display, spray tanned to bronzed perfection.

"Mind if join you?" he asked, flashing me his pearly whites.

"Of course not, come on in."

At last, a friendly face.

A little too friendly, as things turned out.

"How's it going, June?" he said, immersing himself in the bubbles.

Before I had a chance to reply, he inched closer to me and cooed, "Anyone ever tell you you look mighty fetching in a bathing suit?"

(His eyes, I might point out, were nowhere near the ghastly loaner bathing suit I'd donned, but rather on my bobbing cleavage.)

"Only my mother," I said, sidling away from him, "and I was seven at the time."

"Ha ha," he said, closing the gap between us. "I love a self-deprecating woman."

Frankly, I was surprised he knew the meaning of self-deprecating.

"After we finish our little soak," he asked, flashing me his idea of bedroom eyes, "how about we head up to my room for a shower?"

Yikes. The guy was about as subtle as a sledge-hammer.

"So what do you say, June?"

"I don't think so," I demurred.

To be perfectly honest, he wasn't my type. As you well know from my encounters with Darryl, I much prefer a sensitive sweetie to a muscle-bound gym rat whose idea of foreplay is looking at his own head shots. And even if Clint were my type, I try never to have dipsy doodle with some-one who can't remember my name. Call me wacky, but that's usually a deal breaker.

I scooted away a few inches. And once more, he wasted no time closing the gap between us. By now we'd made a full circle around the jacuzzi and Clint was beginning to get ticked off.

"Don't you understand?" He pouted. "I'm giving you the opportunity to make world class love with a major motion picture star."

"Really? Who?"

Okay, I didn't really say that. It's just that when I think of major motion picture stars, I think of guys like George Clooney and Cary Grant. Not the steroid-injected lunkhead who ran around in a loin cloth in *Revenge of the Lust Busters.*

"Actually, I'm very flattered that you want to, um, 'take a shower' with me, Clint, but I can't. I'm just too upset about Mallory's murder. I practically discovered her body, you know."

Suddenly he remembered he was supposed to be in mourning.

"Oh, right." He slapped on a suitably soulful expression. "Poor Mallory. Strangled with a piece of seaweed. What an awful way to go!" He shook his head in faux sorrow. "Such a great gal. Although," he said, doing surreptitious leg kicks in the water, "she really did have a habit of making enemies. Not me, of course," he hastened to add. "I always loved her."

Man, this guy was one heck of a stinky actor. I'd seen better performances from the clown at the Jack in the Box.

"Do you have any idea who might have done it?"

"None whatsoever. Like I told the police, I was in my room the entire time."

"So you saw nothing and heard nothing?"

"All I heard was Shawna and Sven arguing in the gym."

"You heard them from your room?"

"Oh, yes. My balcony faces the back of the estate and their voices carried."

So The Aerobic Twins hadn't been lying about being at the gym at the time of the murder. That still didn't mean Shawna couldn't have taken time out to strangle Mallory, but it certainly shoved her a bit lower on my suspect list.

"You should have heard Shawna reaming into Sven. She said she was sick and tired of his fooling around and that she couldn't believe he was stupid enough to get involved with a woman like Mallory. Sooner or later, she said, Sven was bound to get hurt."

Women are amazing, n'est-ce pas? Here Shawna was worried about Sven getting hurt when she was the one who'd just had her heart broken!

"Then Sven said he couldn't help himself, he was overcome by desire; and then he promised he'd never do it again, and that everything would be okay."

"You heard all that from your room?"

Was it my imagination, but was there just a hint of hesitation in his reply?

"Sure," he said. "They were both talking pretty loud. And the sound really carries around here."

Not really.

Those of you taking notes will no doubt recall my hellish stint working in the organic garden, the day I heard Clint begging Mallory not to spill the beans about his ladies' lingerie fetish. I couldn't hear what they were saying. Not at first. I'd had to scoot closer to the house to listen in.

Maybe Shawna and Sven had been shouting loud enough for the sound to carry.

Then again, maybe Clint just happened to hear them as he walked past the gym on his way back from strangling Mallory.

*   *   *

All that chatter about Mallory's murder must've taken the starch out of Clint's Speedo, because he soon bid me a hasty farewell and returned to his room, presumably to shower alone.

I looked around the pool area and saw that Harvy and Kendra were gone, too.

I was tempted to haul myself out of the jacuzzi and see if they left behind any pretzels, but I was too lazy to move. All that hot water was making me sleepy.

And before long I drifted off into a most delicious doze, starring me and my favorite dream co-star, George Clooney.

This time George and I were lounging beachside in a tropical paradise, George as stunning as ever in sedate but sexy swim trunks, me in a string bikini, my thighs miraculously thin.

And here's the best part: George was hand feeding me pretzels dipped in Chunky Monkey ice cream!

It was heaven. Sheer heaven.

And then, abruptly, as things tend to happen in dreams, Darryl of Darryl's Deli came racing up to us on the beach.

"Jaine, what are you doing here with George Clooney?" he asked, a look of consternation in his definitely-hazel eyes.

"She's eating ice cream and pretzels, buddy," George said. "Want to make something of it?"

"I sure do," Darryl cried. "You can't stay here Jaine!"

"Sez who?" George said, getting up.

"Sez me, that's who!" Darryl replied, fire in those hazel eyes.

Oh, wow! Geo. Clooney and Darryl of Darryl's Deli were fighting over me, Jaine Austen. This was even better than the ice cream and pretzels. Almost.

"C'mon, Jaine," Darryl said, pulling me up from the sand. "You've got to get out of here."

"Why? Can't you two keep fighting over me just a little while longer? At least until I run out of pretzels."

"Don't you remember what happened the last time you were in a dream with George Clooney?" Darryl said. "Someone got murdered!"

Omigosh, he was right.

"You'd better wake up ASAP."

I tried to force myself awake, but I was trapped in the dream. And what's worse, George and Darryl had vanished. Suddenly I was no longer on the beach, but in the ocean, under water, the waves churning around me. I tried to push up to the surface, but something was holding me down.

And then I realized this was no dream. This was really happening!

I was still in the jacuzzi, and someone was trying to drown me!

I thrashed and kicked to no avail. Oh, God, the water was coming up my nose. And then, just as suddenly as it had started, the hands that were holding me down released me.

Coughing and gasping for air, I came bursting up out of the water.

After I'd finally managed to catch my breath, I looked around to see who'd attacked me. But whoever had done it was long gone.

I stumbled out of the jacuzzi and wrapped myself in my spa robe, shivering in spite of all that hot water I'd been soaking in.

On shaky legs, I headed up the path to the main house.

For a minute I wondered if maybe I had dreamed the whole thing, after all. Had I simply fallen asleep and slipped underwater?

No, it couldn't be. I'd felt those hands on my head, pushing me down. They were real, all right.

And that could mean only one thing.

The killer had struck again.

Chapter 21

I skipped cocktail hour that night, opting instead to cower in bed, curled in a fetal position.

"Oh, Pro," I moaned, burrowing under the covers, "someone tried to drown me in the jacuzzi! It was awful, just awful! All that water in my nose! I couldn't breathe! I honestly thought I was going to die!"

Prozac, who had been napping on her treadmill, scurried to my side, shooting me a mooney-eyed look that could mean only one thing:

Thank God you're still alive! Now you can go out to the car and get me some more cat food.

With that, she began her patented Feed Me dance on the bedspread.

Oh, groan. How was I going to break it to her? There *was* no more cat food.

"Pro, sweetie," I said, scratching her favorite spot behind her ears. "I'm so sorry. All I bought

was one emergency can, and you already ate it.
But I promise I'll run into town and get you another right after dinner."

Her eyes widened in disbelief.

*Just one emergency can? And you call yourself a cat
owner?*

I thought for sure I was in for a major yowl-
fest, but once she realized there was no chow
forthcoming, she just stalked out to the patio,
her tail swishing in irritation.

I resumed my fetal position, staring at some
water stains on the ceiling, cursing the day I'd
ever checked into The Haven. Maybe I should
call a halt to my investigation and wait for
Brangelina to find the culprit on their own. But
Lord only knew how long that would take—and
how many more three-hundred calorie meals I
would have to suffer through.

Besides, I couldn't let the killer intimidate me.
I'd be a disgrace to part-time semi-professional
P.I.s everywhere.

No, I'd hang tough and pick up where I'd left
off.

And so, after treating myself to a hot shower—
and an Altoid that had escaped Olga's eagle
eye—I left Prozac out on the patio, and joined
my fellow murder suspects for dinner.

"So who did it?" I asked Cathy, as I sat beside
her at the "B" table. "Who killed Mallory?"

When we last left Cathy, if you recall, she was
convinced she'd figured out who the killer was.

"Well," she said, carefully selecting a radish

from our crudite plate, "at first I was sure it was her ex-husband. I read in the tabloids they went through a really messy divorce."

"But doesn't he live in Australia?" I asked, remembering the down under hunk Mallory had been married to for about fifteen minutes.

"Yes," she conceded. "And on the day of the murder he was supposedly shooting a movie on location in Sydney. But I figured maybe he got a stunt double to take his place while he flew to the States on a private jet and strangled Mallory. But the more I thought of it, the more it seemed a bit far-fetched, huh?"

"Maybe just a tad."

"Then I figured it had to be Kendra. Anyone could see she hated her sister's guts. But then, Olga hated Mallory, too, for threatening to ruin The Haven. And Harvy must've been furious when Mallory decided to stop payment on his check. And just when I was convinced Harvy did it, I thought of Shawna. Surely she felt like strangling Mallory, the way she'd been making a play for Sven."

Yadda yadda, blah blah. Tell me something I hadn't already thought of.

"But now," she announced, waving her radish with a flourish, "I'm pretty sure I know who did it, after all."

"Who?"

"Delphine," she nodded smugly.

"The maid? Why on earth would Delphine want to kill Mallory?"

But I didn't get to find out why, because just then Olga came marching over with our fresh weed salads, tossed as usual, in a piquant Pine-Sol dressing.

"Eat hearty, gals," she said, dumping the plates in front of us.

"Looks yum!" said Cathy, the little toady.

"So why did Delphine kill Mallory?" I repeated in a hushed whisper, the minute the Diet Nazi had goose-stepped away.

"Oh, I haven't figured out that part yet," Cathy replied breezily, "but Delphine's such a sneak, I wouldn't put anything past her."

Right, Cath. When solving a mystery, who needs a pesky little thing like a motive?

"Delphine is just like Dawn Drummond," she said, spearing her weeds with gusto.

"Dawn Drummond?"

"A gal I work with at the Piggly Wiggly." Cathy lowered her voice to a whisper, as if about to impart classified military secrets. "I personally have seen Dawn spill ketchup on a *People* magazine during her lunch break, and then put it back on the magazine rack!"

I did my best to look horrified.

"The woman is utterly unscrupulous. The week she was in charge of watering the Christmas poinsettias, three of them died!"

As she rambled on about Dawn's many foibles, I let my gaze wander to the "A" table, where Harvy, Kendra, and Clint were sneaking shots of booze from a flask. Indeed they were feeling no pain, giggling like naughty school kids, hiding the flask when Olga came out from the kitchen, then whipping it out when she went back in.

The few times they glanced in my direction, it

was not, I regret to inform you, with a jolly wave, or to ask me if I'd care for a wee bit 'o booze. Indeed, I seemed to be high on their Most Likely to be Shunned for All Eternity list.

Dinner slogged on. Our Pine-Sol salads were whisked away, replaced by the main course—pork loin ala Kevin. Which is to say, a most depressing shade of gray. Stylish, perhaps, on a Prada suit. Not so hot on a piece of pork. I picked at it listlessly, wondering how Kevin managed to decolorize absolutely everything he cooked.

Meanwhile Cathy was still on a toot about Disgraceful Dawn—yammering about her deplorable habit of pilfering grapes from the produce section—when I happened to glance up and see something that made my blood freeze.

There, prancing out in the lobby before my horrified eyes, was Prozac.

And she was not alone. No, sir. Dangling from her mouth was one of Olga's prized koi!

When I'd left my room earlier, she'd been hunched up on the patio chaise staring out into the distance. I should've known she'd been eyeing that koi. Somehow she'd managed to bust out of stir and go for her prey!

"Omigod!" I moaned.

"I know," Cathy tsked. "It's disgraceful, isn't it? Not only is she stealing produce, but she eats the grapes without washing them. Ugh!"

Thank heavens Cathy was facing away from the hallway, so she hadn't noticed my little fishnapper. Nor had the gang at the "A" table, still busy sneaking shots from their flask.

"I just remembered a very important call I have to make," I said, jumping up.

"But you'll miss dessert," Cathy protested. "Tonight it's gluten-free zucchini cookies."

"Mighty tempting," I said, dashing for the door, "but I'll pass."

I got to the lobby just in time to see Prozac's tail disappearing into the lounge. Lunging in after her, I spotted her near the fireplace, the poor koi still flapping in her mouth. For a terrifying instant, I was afraid she was going to toss it into the flames for a quickie barbeque.

But no, the minute she saw me, she was off and running again.

Damn that cat. She was actually enjoying this!

And it was at that moment, just as I was about to take off after her, that a tiny ball of tan fur came whizzing into the room.

Good heavens, it was Armani! He'd seen Prozac and Mr. Fish and had decided to join in the fun.

So there we were in a frantic daisy chain, me chasing Armani while Armani chased Prozac while the poor little koi was no doubt wondering what the heck had happened to his pond.

Fortunately, thanks to all those years of being toted around in the crook of Mallory's arm, Armani wasn't used to high speed chases, and I quickly managed to nab him. Frantic, I looked around for a place to stash him.

Spotting a nearby door, I opened it and saw a small well-appointed library, filled to the brim with leather bound volumes.

"No fish for you," I hissed, tossing him inside. Then, firmly shutting the door, I returned to Prozac, who continued to lead me on a merry chase around the furniture, her tail swishing with glee. It seemed like forever but was probably only seconds before I caught up with her behind a loveseat, where she dropped the fish at my feet.

Quite proud of herself.

I'd like it sauteed, please, with a beurre blanc.

I looked down at the poor critter. Thank heavens it was still wriggling. Thrilled to see no visible blood, I snatched it up with one hand, and with Prozac slung under my other arm, I raced back to my room where I filled my sink with water, and dropped in the fish.

Prozac looked up from where she was pacing at my ankles.

Wait a minute. That's not beurre blanc.

I stared at the sink in dismay. The koi was just floating there, immobile. Oh, Lord. It was dead after all. Desperate, I gave it a gentle push.

And then—miraculously—my little gold friend started swimming!

Hallelujah! It was still alive! As I watched it circumnavigate the sink, my heart flooded with relief.

But just when my blood pressure was descending from the stratosphere, I remembered Armani.

I raced downstairs to the library where I found him busily chewing a first edition of *The Catcher in the Rye*. I wrestled it away from him

(I've still got the commemorative scars to prove it) and was just putting the book back on the shelf when Kendra came wandering in.

"I've been looking for you everywhere!" she scolded Armani. "What the heck have you been up to?

"Catching up on his reading," I said with a feeble laugh, hoping she wouldn't notice the scrap of J.D. Salinger hanging from his tush.

Unwilling to risk any surprise encounters, I decided to wait until everyone had gone to bed to put Mr. Koi back in his pond. Which meant I spent the next hellish few hours trying to keep Prozac out of the bathroom and away from her "dinner."

At one point she gave up on the bathroom and made a mad dash for the patio screen. For the first time I noticed a gap in the bottom of the mesh. So that's how the little devil made her escape. I had no idea if the opening had been there all along, or if my ingenious kitty had managed to pry it open herself. I wouldn't put it past her. This was a cat who could crack open a safe if there was something to nosh on inside.

Before she could escape again, I grabbed her and deposited her on the bed, locking the door to the patio.

The minutes passed like centuries as she yowled for her lost dinner.

I was tempted to run to town to get her some cat food, but I couldn't trust her with the koi just a bathroom away. So I stuck it out until I was fairly certain everyone had retired for the night.

And then I got ready for my mission.

Looking around my room, I spotted the bowl of fresh flowers on my dresser. I dumped out the flowers and rinsed the bowl in the bathtub, filling it with fresh water. Then I scooped up the koi, still doing laps in the sink—and plopped the poor little thing into the bowl.

"C'mon, sweetpea," I said. "We're going home."

I tiptoed down the corridor with my precious cargo, praying I wouldn't bump into Olga on her way to the kitchen for a midnight snack.

My prayers were answered, and I was soon slipping out the back door and along the path to the koi pond.

"Okay, little fella," I said when I reached my destination, "time to join your brothers and sisters."

I was just about to preside over this touching family reunion, when I heard a chirpy voice behind me say:

"Bon voyage!"

I whirled around to see Delphine, still in uniform, arms clamped across her flat chest.

"What's up?" she asked with a sly grin.

Oh, foo. What on earth was I going to tell her?

"A gift for Olga," I lied shamelessly, dropping the fish in the pond. "I was in town today and picked up another koi for her collection."

"Really?" she smirked. "The same koi I saw in your cat's mouth earlier this evening?"

Rats. Busted.

But I'd be damned if I was going to let her rattle my nerves.

"Okay, so my cat took the fish," I said, going for an air of nonchalance. "It's alive and that's all that matters."

"Not exactly," Delphine pointed out. "Olga's crazy about her koi babies. If she knew Sparky had almost been cat food, she'd have a snit fit."

"Sparky?"

"Yes, she's got names for all of them. Sparky's the one with the black dots down his back."

Oh, Lordy. Who knew that Olga was a koi cuckoo? I hated to think what she'd do to me if she found out about Prozac's fishnapping. Probably chain me 24/7 to that damn organic garden.

"You're not going to tell her, are you?" I asked, unable to keep a pleading note from my voice.

"Of course not," she assured me. "I won't breathe a word."

"You won't?"

"Worry not. For fifty bucks, my lips are sealed forever."

Oh, for crying out loud. She'd be blackmailing me about this for the rest of my life.

And suddenly something in me snapped. I'd had it up to here with this pint-sized con artist.

"Go ahead and blab to Olga! And I'll tell her how you're selling forbidden calories to her guests. You'll be out of a job before you can say 'highway robbery.'"

But if I expected her to be cowed, I was sadly mistaken.

"Olga will never fire me," she said. "Not with what I know."

"What do you know?"

"I know," she said, pausing for dramatic effect, "that Olga killed Mallory."

"What??"

"It's true," she insisted. "Right about the time Mallory was killed, I happened to be taking a teensy break from my chores and sampling the pinot noir in Harvy's minibar. Anyhow, I was looking out Harvy's window when I saw Olga come running out of the spa therapy center. She dashed out of there like a crazy lady, her eyes all buggy and weird. Like ... well, like she'd just strangled someone."

Oh, boy. It looked like Olga had just joined the rapidly swelling ranks of my Most Likely Suspects.

"She killed Mallory all right," Delphine nodded confidently. "Olga wasn't about to let that bitch destroy The Haven with her gossip. So you can tell her all about my little food concession. She's not about to fire me. Not with what I know.

"But you, on the other hand," she said, that smirk of hers back in action, "she's not scared of you at all. Quite the contrary."

She held out her palm.

"So that'll be fifty bucks, please."

You'll be quite proud to know that I stuck to my guns and refused to fork over fifty bucks for her silence.

I did, however, fork over fifty bucks for some M&N's and a can of Fancy Feast, which the little extortionist just happened to have in her pockets.

Fifty bucks richer, Delphine skipped off into the night, leaving me alone at the koi pond. I stood there watching Sparky frolic with his kin, cursing Delphine and, not incidentally, wondering if The Haven's genial Diet Nazi was indeed a killer.

YOU'VE GOT MAIL

To: Jausten
From: DaddyO
Subject: Not My Fault!!

I don't care what Mom says about the debate, it
was not my fault.

Your innocent,

Daddy

To: Jausten
From: Shoptillyoudrop
Subject: So Mad I Could Spit!

I'm so mad at Daddy I could spit. You won't
believe what happened at the debate.

First off, he insisted on taking one of his dratted
gnomes with him, as a "visual aid." I had to hold
the hideous creature in my lap as we drove over to
the clubhouse. Daddy made such a fuss over the
darn thing, I'm surprised he didn't buy it a car seat.

Anyhow, we got to the clubhouse and were
walking past the rec room when Daddy poked his
head inside and saw the remains of a party buffet.

"Oh, wow!" Daddy said, eyeing one of the platters.
"Baby lamb chops! My favorite."

"Hank Austen!" I said. "Don't you dare go in there and take one of those lamb chops."

"Why on earth not?" he wanted to know.

"First, because it's not our food, and second, because we don't have time. The debate is scheduled to start any minute."

"Oh, please," Daddy pshawed, "they can't start the debate without me. Besides, I'm starving."

"Starving? You just finished a meatloaf dinner!"

But you know Daddy. Nothing I ever say makes a dent in that brain of his. Before I could stop him, he was zooming over to the buffet table for a baby lamb chop. Which I have to confess was quite tasty. (Okay, I had one myself).

And then, just as he was reaching for another, the most awful thing happened.

With that dratted gnome in his arms, he knocked over a glass of champagne, which spilled right down the front of his pants!

In a most embarrassing spot.

"Oh, for heavens sakes!" I said. "Now look what you've done. You can't go walking around like you've just taken a tinkle in your pants."

Instead of worrying like a normal person, Daddy just smiled in that superior way of his and said, "That's the trouble with you, honeybun. You panic in times of crisis. While I, on the other hand, stay cool as a cucumber. That's one of the key leadership qualities I possess that will make me such a valuable president of the homeowners association."

"Okay, Mr. President, exactly what do you intend to do?"

"Simple. I'll dry my pants under the men's room hand dryer. They'll be good as new before you can say, You Can Bank on Hank For President!"

And with that, he shoved the gnome in my arms and dashed across the hallway to the men's room.

Well, honey, I stood outside that men's room for what seemed like a small eternity when suddenly I heard Daddy shout, "Oh no!"

Two seconds later, he poked his head out the door.

"What on earth happened?" I asked.

"I set my pants on fire."

"What??"

It turns out he held the pants way too close to the dryer nozzle and I guess it must have ignited the alcohol from the champagne.

"Now what are we going to do?" he wailed. "I had to throw my pants in the trash."

At which point Artie Myers came running up to us.

"Where the hell have you been, Hank? The debate was supposed to start five minutes ago."

Daddy explained how he'd set his pants on fire, and I offered to go back home and get another pair.

"We don't have time for that," Artie said. "I've got a poker game that starts in a half hour. Let's get this show on the road."

So we hustled up the stairs to the Channel 99 studio, with Daddy in his *I ♥ My Gnome* boxer shorts, praying no one would see us.

"Don't worry," Artie told Daddy when we got to the studio. "Just stand behind the podium, and I'll shoot you from the waist up."

I waited in the wings as Daddy took his spot behind one of his coffin shaped podiums, his gnome on the floor beside him. Then the cameras started rolling and the debate began. Lydia, needless to say, after an initial gasp at Daddy's boxers, was poise personified, talking about her plans to improve the quality of life at Tampa Vistas.

Then it was Daddy's turn to speak. Up to this point, Daddy had been Mr. Confident, snickering and smirking throughout Lydia's wonderful speech. But the minute the camera was on him, he froze. Just stood there and gulped.

Finally, he took out his notes, cleared his throat and said, "And now, a few words about ancient Aztec and Incan civilizations. . . ."

Good heavens! He'd taken my class notes by mistake!

I couldn't believe it. I'd spent all day listening to him rehearse his speech about freedom of speech and press and the right to bear lawn gnomes. And here he was yakking about how the Aztecs invented popcorn!

We all just stood there, boggled, wondering what on earth had gotten into him. Then I guess Daddy must have realized he was several hundred years and a hemisphere off topic, and began blathering about his campaign to save the gnomes.

Finally, remembering his visual aid, he picked up his gnome and said, "I'd like you to meet a little friend of mine."

He plunked the gnome down on the podium. And that's when it all fell apart. Literally. The minute the gnome hit the podium, the rickety wooden structure shattered to smithereens. Which was no surprise. The darn thing had been practically put together with spit and paper clips. And that silly gnome weighed a ton.

So there was Daddy, without a podium for cover, in his *I ♥ My Gnome* boxers, his own "little friend" *thisclose* to making its TV debut.

And as if that weren't bad enough, the very next minute the janitor came racing in the studio shouting, "Everybody out! Fire in the clubhouse! Some idiot put a pair of burning pants in the trash!"

Not only did Daddy expose himself in his underwear to all of Tampa Vistas, the darn fool set fire to the clubhouse men's room!

In other words, honey, I think it's safe to say that

HANK STANK!

And as for me, I've never been so humiliated in all my life!

Love and kisses from

Your wretched,

Mom

To: Jausten
From: Sir Lancelot
Subject: Surely You Didn't Mean It

Jaine, sweetie, I got your last message and I must say I was rather upset. Surely you didn't mean it when you threatened to choke me with a chimichanga.

I'm sorry if you resent a few meals I might have enjoyed while you were dieting. I never dreamed it would get on your nerves.

I'm sure you're just cranky from all that sugar withdrawal.

Hug hug, kiss kiss,

Lance

PS. Will call soon. I promise!

Chapter 22

I cringed at the thought of questioning the Diet Nazi about Mallory's murder. (You would, too, if you'd seen her biceps.) But question her I must, so I decided to use my busted patio screen as an excuse to pay her a little visit.

I waited till after breakfast the next morning (rice cakes and stewed prunes—gaaack!), and found her office tucked away at the back of The Haven across from the kitchen. At least I assumed it was her office from the PRIVATE sign on the door.

The door was partially open, and after a tentative knock, I poked my head inside.

Olga, seated behind a desk, waved me in as she talked on the phone.

"I can assure you, Mrs. Washton," she was cooing, "that Mallory Francis's tragic demise has not affected the safety of our guests in the slightest."

Yeah, right. Except for the occasional attempted jacuzzi drowning.

As Olga rambled on about the nonexistent security system at The Haven, I glanced around her small office, which was decorated more like a living room than a place of business, with furniture straight out of the pages of *Architectural Digest*. True, it would have been a decades old issue of the magazine. But even I, the queen of Ikea, could tell the stuff had cost a bundle in its day.

Through an open doorway I caught a glimpse of an adjoining bedroom.

So this was where Olga lived.

Scattered on a nearby étagère were several sterling-framed photos of Olga in better days, arm in arm with a distinguished older man. Probably her deceased husband. In one picture they were sitting on a sofa in front of the fireplace in the lounge. Back when it was their living room, and not a gathering place for paying guests.

To think this vast estate was once Olga's private residence, and now she was reduced to living in two cramped rooms.

No wonder she was such a grouch.

Then another picture caught my eye. A publicity shot of Olga, back when she was a wannabe starlet. I was stunned by how sweet she looked, no trace of hardness in her blue eyes or wide smile. Her thick blond hair, unbound from Valkyrie braids, flowed freely to her shoulders.

She'd been a beauty, all right. Every bit as pretty as Mallory.

Surely she must have resented Mallory's rise to fame. Enough, I wondered, to propel her to murder?

Behind me I could hear her grow more desperate as she tried to keep her skittish customer from jumping ship.

"Honestly, Mrs. Washton, you and your poodle will be perfectly safe during your stay. . . . Why don't I give you a twenty-five percent discount as a show of good faith? . . . Fifty percent? . . . And extra dog treats for Tinkerbell?" Then a deep sigh. "Well, I'm sorry you feel that way. Maybe some other time."

She hung up with a groan and raked her fingers through her hair, unleashing rebel tendrils from her braids.

"If this keeps up, I should be out of business by next Tuesday."

"I'm sure the police will find the killer soon," I offered feebly.

At which point she remembered I was one of her inmates.

"Shouldn't you be in aerobics class?" she scowled.

"I just popped by to tell you there's a rip in my patio screen."

"Okay," she nodded. "I'll take care of it. Anything else?"

You bet there was something else.

"You may have heard," I said, clearing my throat, "that I've been making some inquiries into Mallory's death."

By now I figured the whole world knew.

"Shawna mentioned you were some kind of P.I., but I thought she was joking."

I forged ahead, choosing to ignore that zinger.

"Like I said, I've been investigating the murder. It was pretty horrible the way Mallory was strangled, huh?"

"I can't pretend I liked the bitch, but she certainly didn't deserve to die like that."

"Lucky thing she went when she did, though."

"What do you mean by that?" she asked, flexing her biceps in a manner that made me distinctly uneasy.

"Only that if Mallory had lived, she might have made good on her threat to ruin The Haven."

"Wait a minute, honey." She got up from behind her desk, a forbidding figure in denim overalls and Gestapo work boots. "You're not accusing me of killing Mallory, are you?"

I edged closer to the étagère, figuring I could always bop her over the head with one of her sterling frames if she attacked me.

"Um . . . now that you mention it," I stammered, "I have it on good authority that you were seen running out of the spa therapy center around the time of Mallory's murder."

"What good authority?"

I didn't like the way that vein in her neck was throbbing.

"It doesn't matter. All that matters is that you were seen at the scene of the crime."

I reached for one of the frames, just in case of

violence, but much to my relief, no fisticuffs en-
sued.

"Okay," she sighed, slumping down into a
nearby armchair, "so I went to Mallory's cubicle.
I was going to throw myself on her mercy and
beg her not to trash The Haven. But I swear she
was dead when I got there."

She looked up at me with those still beautiful
blue eyes, and there was something in them that
made me want to believe her.

"So I panicked and ran. And then when
Shawna discovered the body, I decided to keep
my mouth shut and pretend I'd never been
there. But I can assure you," she said, the starch
returning to her spine, "you are barking up the
wrong suspect. I did not kill Mallory Francis."

I looked around her tiny living room, crammed
with relics of a happier life, and at that moment,
in spite of all the hell Olga had put me through,
I couldn't help feeling a spark of pity for her.

"Who was it who saw me at the spa therapy
center, anyway?" she asked.

Ordinarily I wouldn't want to cause trouble
between an employee and her boss, but in Delphine's case, I was willing to make an exception.
Frankly, I was surprised the little extortionist
hadn't already tried blackmailing Olga for her
silence.

"It was Delphine."

"Why, that rat!" she cried, banging her fist
down on her desk. "I knew the kid was trouble
the minute I hired her. She refuses to do hospital corners on the sheets. Can't fold a towel to

save her life. Sells food to the customers behind my back—"

"You know about that?"

"Of course I do. I'd fire her in a minute, but I can't find anybody to work that cheap. So I've put up with her food cart, her affair with Sven, her goofing off on the job—"

"Whoa. Back up a sec. What affair with Sven?"

Olga rolled her eyes in disgust.

"Delphine wasn't here two weeks before she was making a play for him. Bragged about it to me. Said Sven was going to leave Shawna to marry her. But that all stopped when Mallory showed up. He dropped Delphine like a hot potato."

Holy Mackerel. That sound you just heard was yet another suspect popping up. Was it possible Delphine bumped off Mallory?

Maybe she hadn't been in Harvy's room when she saw Olga running from the spa therapy center. Maybe she'd been hiding nearby in the shrubs, just waiting for her chance to race in and bump off her rival for Sven's affections.

"Now that I think of it," Olga said, interrupting my thoughts, "that gives Delphine a motive to kill Mallory, doesn't it?"

For once, the Diet Nazi and I were on the same page.

In a burst of defiance, I did not go to aerobics class. Instead, I decided to have a little chat with my Merry Maid from Hell.

I roamed around until I found her in Clint's room. At least I assumed it was Clint's room, from the barbells on the floor and the *Victoria's Secret* catalog on the night stand.

Delphine was not, as you might imagine, busy making the bed or dusting the armoire. Rather she was stretched out on said bed watching *The Price is Right*, munching on some M&N's. And draped around her neck was a hot pink feather boa.

"Ahem." I cleared my throat to let her know she had company.

Muting the TV, she looked up at me with mild curiosity, not the least bit guilty about having been caught goofing off.

"Shouldn't you be in aerobics?"

"Shouldn't *you* be vacuuming?"

"I decided to take a break," she shrugged. "How do you like the boa?" She ran her fingers over the pink feathers. "Yummy, isn't it? I found it in Clint's dresser."

With that, she got up and sashayed around the room, working the boa like a seasoned stripper, which heaven knows she might well have been.

"You should see what fabulous teddies he has!"

Without batting an eyelash, she opened one of Clint's dresser drawers and took out a gossamer confection of creamy lace, holding it up in front of her.

"If only we were the same size," she sighed, tossing it back in the drawer.

"Do you make a practice of snooping in other people's drawers?" I asked, bristling with righteous indig.

"Sure do. Gotta have some fun at this crummy job. By the way, you could use some new undies."

For crying out loud. The kid had all the scruples of a hedge fund manager.

"Thanks. I'll keep that in mind."

"So what can I do you for?" she asked, plopping back onto Clint's bed, her dirty sneakers on his duvet cover. "I'm running a special on American cheese sandwiches. Just thirty bucks and I throw in a bag of chips."

Tempted as I was to spring for some chips, I managed to restrain myself and get down to the business at hand.

"I know all about your affair with Sven," I announced.

"So?" She picked up Clint's *Victoria's Secret* catalog, and flipped a page.

"So I know you were crazy about him and wanted to marry him. But then Mallory came along and ruined everything."

"Me? Crazy about Sven?" She barked out a brittle laugh. "That's nuts. I was just in it for the blazing mattresses. I knew he'd never leave Shawna. Sven's practically got an umbilical cord attached to his abs.

"Besides," she sniffed, "I'm not about to wind up with some tacky aerobics instructor. When I settle down, the guy's gonna have an '–illionaire' at the end of his name."

"So it didn't bother you when Sven began fooling around with Mallory?"

"Oh, please. I couldn't care less."

She went back to reading *Victoria's Secret*, doing her best to look cool and collected. And it would have worked, too.

If she hadn't been reading it upside down.

Oh, she was bothered, all right. Maybe even enough to have strangled the life out of Mallory.

I was heading for the door, wondering if I could possibly nab a bag of chips en route, when Delphine called out to me.

"I wouldn't go around spreading rumors, Jaine. I once read about a woman who spread rumors, and she wound up strangled with her own elastic-waist pants."

To drive home her point, she tightened the boa around her neck.

"Get my drift?"

Did I ever.

Next thing I knew, she'd be leaving a horse's head in my bed.

And charging me for it.

Chapter 23

Olga stayed barricaded in her office the rest of the afternoon, no doubt trying to stem the tide of customers canceling their reservations. If she had indeed murdered Mallory to save her spa, it looked like her plan had backfired.

So I took advantage of the Diet Nazi's absence to hole up in my room with Prozac and a supply of snacks I picked up on an emergency run to Darryl's. In spite of my stern lecture to myself the other night, I'd been hoping to run into my deli doll, but was disappointed to see a strange clerk at the counter. Oh, well. What did it matter? Darryl wasn't interested in me anyway.

Time to focus on the murder.

By now my head was spinning with suspects. Everywhere I turned, a new one seemed to pop to the top of my Most Likely list. What I needed was to sort things out in my mind. And at times like this it often helps to write out the facts of the case.

So after a nourishing snack of peanut butter on Ritz crackers, I hunkered down with my laptop. Unfortunately I made the mistake of checking my e-mails first. You'd think by now I would have learned to Just Say No to anything from Shoptillyoudrop and DaddyO. But like a freeway rubbernecker unable to avert her eyes from an accident, I just had to find out what happened next in the disaster-thon known as my parents' lives.

Gaak! Can you believe Daddy showing up on TV in his *I ♥ My Gnome* boxer shorts? Not to mention setting fire to the men's room!

It's a wonder he hasn't been exiled to Boca Raton.

But I couldn't think about Daddy now. After a tad more peanut butter (it's a protein, you know), I bit the bullet and wrote out my suspect list.

Here's what I came up with:

My Suspects

By Jaine Austen

KENDRA FRANCIS. *Mallory's doormat of a sister. After years of abuse, had she finally snapped? Hoping to inherit a bundle, had she tossed her drugged tea outside her cubicle window and strangled her sister with a piece of kelp? Were those* scratches I'd seen on her chest really from Armani, or from Mallory fighting for her life?

HARVY. Mallory's personal hairstylist and head cheerleader. Mallory was about to pull the plug on the salon of his dreams. According to Shawna, he was missing from his cubicle at the time of Mallory's murder. Was he back in his room, as he claimed, getting an aspirin? Or across the hall with Mallory, strangling the life out of his boss from hell?

SVEN. Studmuffin aerobics instructor with the morals of an alley cat. Cheating on his wife with both Mallory and Delphine. And Lord knows how many others. Clearly a rat of the highest order. But why would he want to kill Mallory? He was the one person at The Haven having fun with her.

SHAWNA. Sven's long-suffering wife. Says she was in the gym arguing with Sven while the murder took place. But she could have easily slipped into Mallory's cubicle to strangle her rival in romance with a deadly hunk of kelp.

CLINT MASTERS. Cross-dressing macho action superstar. Mallory was about to the spill beans about his penchant for ladies lingerie. Says he was in his room at the time of the murder. But who knows if that's true? Maybe he slipped out of his lace teddy and snuck over to the Spa Therapy Center to choke the life out of the woman about to wreck his career.

DELPHINE. The larcenous maid. Semi-threatened to wring my neck with a boa feather. A bit of theatrical bravado? Or had she really meant it? Was my little highway robber a killer, too? Had she wiped out Mallory to save her relationship with Sven? NOTE: Anyone who charges thirty bucks for an American cheese sandwich is a hot suspect in my book.

OLGA. Aka the Diet Nazi. Resented the hell out of her former friend. Swallowed her pride year after year as Mallory showed up at the spa to lord it over her. But then Mallory had threatened to destroy The Haven. Had Olga resorted to murder to save her spa? She admits she was at the scene of the crime, but claims Mallory was already dead when she got there. (Also claims to be a health food nut, but we've seen her swan diving into a Sara Lee. So we can't exactly trust her, can we?)

SARA LEE. Should have picked up some at Darryl's. Why didn't I think of it? Possible to dash out before cocktail hour? Nah, too tired now. Maybe later—

Okay, so my mind wandered. That happens occasionally to us part-time semi-professional P.Is. The important thing is that I'd taken the time to write out my thoughts.

And after carefully reading over my list, one thing was certain—

I still had absolutely no idea who the killer was.

With a weary sigh, I reached for some more peanut butter.

"Yoo hoo, Jaine!"

Cathy's eyes lit up the minute she saw me walk into the lounge for "cocktails." She waved me over to where she was sitting across the room from the others, who were well on their way to getting blitzed on vodka-enhanced celery fizzes.

My tush had barely made contact with the chair when she broke the news.

"I finally figured out who the killer is!"

"Who?"

"Al Qaeda!" she replied in a hushed whisper.

"Al Qaeda? Why on earth would Al Qaeda want to kill Mallory?"

She paused dramatically to pluck a "radish rumaki" from the plate of crudités in front of us.

"Remember in *Revenge of the Lust Busters* how Mallory single-handedly fought off those Arab terrorists, armed with nothing but an emery board and her bullet-proof bustier?"

"Unfortunately, yes."

"Well," Cathy said, chomping down on the rumaki, "I bet Al Qaeda took offense and sent a secret operative to kill her! Makes sense, right?"

Only to a space cadet like Cathy.

"If you ask me, Jaine, I think we should call Homeland Security!"

If you ask me, we should've called the nearest psychiatric ward.

"And I know who it is! The Al Qaeda operative!"

"Who?" I asked warily.

"Clint Masters!"

I looked across the room where Clint was chomping on a carrot stick.

"Clint? A secret terrorist?"

"Yes," she nodded with assurance. "His room is next to mine and the other day I saw him walk out onto his balcony in a long white silky robe. Just like Arab men wear. I could've sworn I saw some sequins on it. But that must have been my imagination."

Oh, Lordy. I couldn't possibly tell her that her Arab terrorist was merely a cross-dresser. The next thing I knew, she'd be blabbing the news to the gang at the Piggly Wiggly and before long it would be all over the tabloids. For all I knew, Clint was a perfectly innocent sexual deviant, and I wasn't about to ruin his career.

"Movie star by day," Cathy was saying, "Al Qaeda operative by night. Don't those guys each get forty virgins for every westerner they kill?"

She clutched my arm in an iron grip.

"My God, Jaine. We could be next! We've got to stick together and never let each other out of our sight!"

Okay, this was where I drew the line. No way was I going to spend the next few days with this delusional talkaholic glued to my side.

"Look, Cathy. I seriously doubt Clint is a member of Al Qaeda."

"Really?"

"Of course! They do all sorts of background checks in the movies. If Clint were a terrorist, they would have found out long ago."

I had no idea if any of this was true, but she seemed to be buying it.

"Gee, I didn't know that." She sighed wistfully, reluctant to give up her role as a Great American Crimefighter. "I guess I'd better cancel Homeland Security, huh?"

"Good idea." I nodded. "Now if you'll excuse

me, I've got an important call I really must make. Catch you at dinner, okay?"

Before she could object, I scooted into the lobby and out the front door, my cell phone glued to my ear, pretending to be talking, just in case she was watching.

Outside, I headed down the main path, past the parking lot, and came across a small wooded lane.

Don't ask me why I decided to go walking down a deserted lane when I knew there was a killer on the loose. Maybe I figured I was safe because three of my top suspects were back in the lounge, scarfing down radish rumakis.

Or maybe my brain was just fried from Cathy's wackadoodle terrorist theories.

Whatever the reason, I put away my phone and began strolling down the lane, surrounded by stately eucalyptus trees.

It felt good to breathe in the fresh, Cathy-free air.

After a few steps, I bent down and picked up a rock. I still had a shred of common sense left, and remembering my near-fatal adventure in the jacuzzi, I wanted to be armed, just in case.

I tried to make good use of my alone time to focus on the murder, but I'm afraid all I could think about was running over to Darryl's after dinner for some Sara Lee cheesecake. I was wandering along, trying to decide between strawberry and cherry topping, when I noticed a cottage up ahead.

Probably an old guest house. Was it possible

Olga lived there and not in those two cramped rooms I'd seen earlier?

Intrigued, I walked up the path to the small Spanish style casita.

From an open window I could hear laughter and soft music. And then the unmistakable sound of Sven crooning, "Oh, babe, you know I'm crazy about you."

Good heavens! Was Sven having an affair with the Diet Nazi?

Quickly, I tiptoed over to the window where the music was coming from and peeked in, eager to see Sven's lover du jour.

Whaddaya know, folks? It was Shawna. This must've been where she and Sven lived. I blinked in amazement to see her lounging on a sofa in shorts and a bikini top.

What astonished me, however, was not Shawna's outfit. (Although I must say, if her shorts were any shorter, they would've been a belt.) No, what caught my eye was the honker emerald pendant nestled in her cleavage.

Yikes! That was Mallory's necklace. What the heck was it doing around Shawna's neck?

Never in a million years would Mallory have given it to her.

I flashed back to the morning I'd seen Sven running out of The Haven, having spent the night with Mallory. At the time I figured all he'd left with were some fond memories of whoopsie doodle, but now I wondered if he'd scampered off with Mallory's pendant, too.

Maybe Mallory found out about it, and threatened to report him to the cops. And maybe, just maybe, Sven had killed her to shut her up.

All along I'd assumed Sven had been ready to dump Shawna for the Hollywood glamour queen. But maybe I was wrong. Maybe he was just playing her, sleeping with her to gain access to her jewels. And maybe Shawna, his long-suffering wife, hadn't been suffering at all. Maybe she was in on the plan from the beginning.

If Shawna had ever been afraid of losing Sven, she sure didn't look it now.

Indeed, she was radiating confidence as she patted a spot on the sofa and said, "C'mere, you."

Sven put down the two champagne glasses he'd been carrying and shimmied in next to her.

"So how do you like it?" he asked, holding the emerald up to the light.

"It's gorgeous," Shawna replied, watching it sparkle. "But you shouldn't have done it."

"Don't worry, babe. Everything's going to be okay now that Mallory's out of the way."

Then he ran his finger along her lush lower lip.

"Love me?"

"You know it."

And with that, she snaked her arm around his neck and drew him in for one steamfest of a kiss.

And it was at that very moment, just as they were sucking the saliva out of each other's innards, that the mood was shattered by the ring tone of a cell phone.

As rotten luck would have it, *my* cell phone.

Why, oh, why hadn't I shut the damn thing off?

I glanced down at the screen and saw Lance's name on the caller ID.

All week, I'd been begging him to call, and *now*, of all times, he was getting back to me. Argggh. Is he impossible, or what?

Jamming the phone in my pocket, I took off like a bat out of hell, praying the love birds hadn't heard anything.

No such luck.

Before long I heard footsteps thundering behind me.

"Catch her, Sven!" Shawna cried.

Thank goodness I'd picked up that rock earlier. Now I turned and hurled it at Sven.

"Damn!" he cried, as it clipped him on his shin.

He stumbled to his knees, and I charged ahead with hope in my heart. I wasn't far from the main path to The Haven; just a few more yards and I'd be out in the open.

But then I felt a rush of wind as Shawna came charging at me and, with linebacker force, tackled me to the ground.

"You silly bitch," she said, sitting astride my chest in her shorts and bikini top. "Why did you have to keep nosing around?"

"Now what are we going to do?" Sven asked, limping toward us, a helpless look on his face.

Clearly Shawna was the brains of this outfit.

"I told you you should have never stolen the

damn emerald," she lashed out at him. "I knew it would turn out to be a disaster."

"I couldn't help myself, hon," he said, shame-faced, like a kid with his hand caught in the cookie jar. "You know how I am."

"Yeah, I know. And one of these days, you're going to get us into trouble I won't be able to fix."

"But what are you going to do about her?" he asked, jerking his head in my direction.

What on earth *was* she going to do? I looked at those strong hands of hers, pinning my arms to the ground.

Any minute now, they'd be around my neck, choking the life out of me.

Oh, God. It was all over. The end. If only I hadn't come to this stupid spa. If only I hadn't gone walking down this stupid lane. If only I'd gone into town for that Sara Lee strawberry or cherry cheesecake—

It was then, just when I was certain I'd eaten my last cheesecake, that I looked up and saw the most beautiful sight in the world:

Chatty Cathy.

Yes, there she was, coming down the lane, my rescuing angel.

"Jaine!" she said, blinking at the tableau before her. "I've been looking all over for you."

"Call 911!" I cried. "Tell them to come quick! And run for your life!"

Cathy's eyes widened in alarm, and as she started running off, Sven lunged after her. But with surprising strength, Cathy hauled off and whacked him aside. I guess all those years toting groceries at the Piggly Wiggly had toughened her up.

I watched her run away, praying Sven and Shawna wouldn't kill me before the cops came.

My prayers were answered.

"C'mon, Sven!" Shawna said, climbing off me. "We gotta clear out—now!"

And before my grateful eyes, they raced back into the woods, leaving me to live another day.

I struggled to my feet and, knees trembling, started back to The Haven.

Thank heavens for Cathy. Who would have thought that jabbering dingbat would wind up saving my life?

How could I ever thank her? Maybe after dinner I'd make an effort to be friendly with her. Sit around and chew the fat about Mr. Muffin, the gang at Piggly Wiggly, her latest terrorist conspiracy theories . . .

Nah. That grateful I wasn't.

Flowers and a thank you note would have to do.

Chapter 24

When Brangelina showed up, they found Sven and Shawna trying to flush Mallory's emerald down the toilet, and wasted no time hauling them off to jail.

Needless to say, I was the center of attention in the aftermath of their arrest. Olga settled me down on a settee as my fellow guests hovered around me in the lounge.

"Tell us everything that happened," Harvy urged, on the edge of his seat, eager for dirt. "Don't leave out a single detail."

"Give the poor thing a chance to catch her breath," Olga said, fluffing a pillow behind my back. "Here, dear. Have a reduced-calorie wine. It'll help you relax."

I took a grateful sip of the wine she handed me, recoiling only slightly at its piquant bouquet of nail polish remover.

"So tell us what happened," Harvy said.

He and Kendra and Clint shot me encouraging smiles. Now that I'd caught the killers, I guess they'd decided I wasn't so bad after all.

And so I began my tale.

But I'd no sooner gotten two sentences out of my mouth, explaining how Sven and Shawna had caught me looking in the window, when Cathy jumped in.

"I knew it was them all along!" she said.

What??? What happened to her "Clint, The Terrorist" theory??

"If it hadn't been for me," she was blathering, "poor Jaine would be dead right now! Luckily I decided to go looking for her, and there she was, lying helplessly on the ground, seconds away from being murdered, I'm sure, when I came to her rescue.

"Seconds away!" she repeated for emphasis. "Not caring a whit for my own safety, I tore Shawna off her, and then when Sven attacked me I had to fight him off with my bare hands, which I never would have been able to do without all the exercises I've learned here at the Haven, which is sort of ironic when you come to think of it. I mean, Sven teaching me exercises that helped me practically knock him out cold."

Wow, if she stretched the truth any further, her nose would start growing.

"Yes, indeed," she said, glowing with pride. "If it weren't for me, poor Jaine would be dead today, and Mallory's killers would still be on the loose!

"Isn't that right, Jaine?"

My cue to shower her with gratitude.

"Absolutely," I said with a stiff smile. "Thank you so much for saving my life."

"Aw, it was nothing," she said, clearly expecting me to order up a ticker tape parade in her honor.

Oh, well, who cared? She *had* saved my life, so I tried my best to keep that smile plastered on my face.

In a burst of democracy, Cathy and I were promoted to the "A" table at dinner that night. Olga bustled around with our salads, thrilled to have Mallory's murder cleared up at last.

"A toast," Harvy said, holding up his lime water, "to Cathy and Jaine, for capturing the killers."

Can you believe it? I was getting second billing to Ms. Yakety-Yak!

"And here's a belated toast to Mallory," Kendra added, raising her glass in a burst of vodka-enhanced goodwill. "I know I've said some pretty horrible things about her. But she was my sister, after all, and a human being—"

"That's debatable," I heard Clint mutter.

"Anyhow, here's to Mallory," Kendra said, "a beautiful woman and a perfectly competent actress who was kind to her dog and gave lots of money to charity even though she only did it for the tax writeoff. I mean, nobody's perfect, right? So what if she tended to alienate everyone she worked with and stepped on a few backs to get ahead? So what if she fired a makeup lady for dropping a pair of false eyelashes and sent some poor guy out to buy mangoes in a hurricane? So what," she said with a tight laugh, "if she treated me like dirt since the time we were toddlers and made me wash her damn pantyhose every goddamn day of her life—"

Whatever goodwill she'd started out with was now gone with the wind.

"Oh, who am I kidding?" she snapped. "She was a vicious bitch, and if you ask me, Sven and Shawna did the world a favor! So here's to Sven and Shawna," she said, slugging down her drink. "May they get time off for good behavior!"

That touching little Kodak moment was interrupted just then by Olga, who came bustling into the room with a dinner tray.

"Special treat, everybody!" she announced. "In honor of Cathy's courageous actions this afternoon, I'm serving double portions of steamed zucchini."

Oh, gaaack.

"And one more thing," Olga added. "I just got off the phone with the police, and you're all free to leave in the morning."

Hallelujah! Suddenly the room was filled with sunshine. Figuratively of course. In fact, it was filled with the stench of steamed zucchini. But you get the idea.

My days in diet hell would soon be over.

At long last, I was going home!

Back in my room, I told Prozac the good news.

"Guess what, Pro? First thing tomorrow, we're outta here!"

Brimming with gratitude, she hurled herself in my arms and licked me with crazed affection.

Okay, so what she really did was look up with a yawn from where she'd been napping.

It's about time. Now how about a belly rub?

When her highness' belly had been rubbed to her satisfaction, I got undressed and fell into bed, conking out the minute my head hit the pillow, exhausted from the day's adventures.

A few hours later I felt a sharp pain in my chest.

No, it was not indigestion from Kevin's ghastly steamed zucchini.

It was Prozac, clawing me awake.

I wanna snack.

And she wasn't the only one. I'd eaten virtually nothing at dinner, so I was feeling a tad peckish myself.

I checked the bedside clock. Eleven thirty. Praying Darryl's was still open, I leaped out of bed and threw on some sweats. I considered slapping on some lipstick and fixing my hair, but quickly nixed that idea, reminding myself that Darryl was simply a friendly deli owner, not my future ex-husband.

Besides, who knew if he'd even be working that night?

As it turned out, he was.

"Hey, there." He grinned as I walked in the door.

I must admit, he looked awfully appealing in a chambray workshirt that brought out the green in his hazel eyes.

Right away I felt my heart go mushy.

Get a grip, Jaine, I told myself. It was just a silly workshirt.

"Picking up some snacks for Grammy?" he asked.

There he was, asking about Grammy again. The guy seemed far more interested in Grammy Austen than he'd ever been in me.

I nodded stiffly and scooted down the aisle, making a beeline for the deli case.

Somehow I managed to perk up at the sight of all the goodies on display.

I chose a gorgeous pastrami and swiss on rye for myself and some extravagantly expensive smoked salmon for Prozac. And if you must know, a teensy weensy Dove Bar for dessert. I'd gathered my loot and was heading for the checkout counter when I stopped cold in my tracks.

There was Cathy, Ms. Goodie Two Shoes Dieter, with enough Snickers bars to feed a small army of chocoholics.

Why, the little hypocrite! After all that holier-than-thou-let's-be-diet-buddies chatter, the woman was your garden variety cheater. And I'd caught her in the act!

Oh, what a wonderful moment! I intended to savor it to the hilt.

"Hi, there, Cath!" I said, strolling up to the checkout counter, all smiles.

She looked down at her stash of chocolate and blushed.

'Got the munchies?" I asked. Somehow I managed not to giggle.

"I may have been cheating just a tad," she said, "what with the stress of Mallory's murder."

"Snickers are her favorite," Darryl pointed out, ringing up her sale.

"You're not going to tell Olga?" Cathy asked, eyes wide with concern. "She'd be so disappointed."

I refrained from telling her that Olga, a woman who sucked cheesecakes straight from the tin, was in no position to pass judgment on anyone's dietary lapses.

"Your secret's safe with me," I assured her.

"Oh, thank you! And I swear I won't tell her that you've been cheating, either," she said, eyeing the goodies in my cart.

And that's when disaster struck.

"Jaine hasn't been cheating," Darryl said. "She's buying all this food for her grandmother."

"Her grandmother?" Cathy blinked, puzzled.

"Sure. Grammy Austen."

"That's crazy. Jaine's rooming with her cat, not her grandmother. Right, Jaine?"

Damn that Cathy and her big fat blabbermouth.

Darryl looked at me, confused. "You're not rooming with your grandmother?"

Oh, Lord. I wanted to fall right through the floor.

"Well, gotta run," Ms. Blabbermouth said, signing her sales receipt, no doubt eager to get started on her Snickers binge. "See you in the morning."

And with that, she grabbed her bag of candy and dashed out the door.

I stared down at the floor, ashamed to face

Darryl, and saw that in her rush to leave, Cathy had dropped her receipt. I picked it up and shoved it in my pocket, figuring I'd give it to her tomorrow. I was too damn angry with Ms. Blabbermouth to go chasing after her now.

Finally I got the courage to make eye contact with Darryl.

"Okay," I sighed. "There is no Grammy Austen. Well, there is, but she's three thousand miles away in her assisted living home in Altoona, Pennsylvania. Cathy was right. My only roommate at The Haven is my cat. I lied because I didn't want you to think I was the kind of woman who goes racing out for pastrami sandwiches and Dove Bars at eleven at night. But I am that kind of woman. I'm a confirmed carbo-holic, I mainline Ben & Jerry, and I'm on a first name basis with my pizza delivery guy."

"Thank God," he sighed.

"You don't mind?"

"Hell, no. When you didn't eat your pizza the other night, I thought you were one of those women who picks at her food."

"You don't like dainty eaters?"

"Are you kidding? My last girlfriend was always on a diet, and it drove me nuts. I want a gal who appreciates food."

"Oh, I've practically got a PhD in Food Appreciation."

"So what's your favorite?" he asked.

"Favorite what?"

"Ben and Jerry. Mine's Chunky Monkey."

Omigod. I swore I heard the sound of bells

ringing. At last I had met my ice cream soul
mate.

"Me, too!" I grinned.

"Listen," he said, suddenly solemn. "I've got a
confession to make. I haven't exactly been honest with you, either. Remember that novel I told
you I was writing?"

"Yes?"

"I've written exactly two words—'Chapter
One.' "

"That's okay. Anyone who can make sandwiches like yours is a creative genius in my
book."

Oh, gosh. There was that killer smile again.

"I don't suppose you'd like to go out with me
the next time I come to L.A?"

Yesyesyesyesyesyesyesyesyesyesyes!

"Sure," I managed to gulp.

Then he came out from behind the counter
in his chambray workshirt and faded jeans.

By now my heart was the consistency of chocolate pudding.

"I wanted to show you our special of the day."

And with that, he took me in his arms and hit
me with the smooch I'd been dreaming of.

All I can say is that when we finally came up
for air, I was one satisfied customer.

I headed to my car, still basking in the glow of
Darryl's kiss. Reaching into my pocket for my
keys, I saw Cathy's sales slip fall out. I picked it
up and was about to shove it back when I saw

something that made me forget all about Darryl and his fabulous lips.

The name on the credit card receipt was not Cathy Kane but Lorraine Sandoval.

Had I picked up someone else's receipt?

No, Cathy's eight Snickers bars were listed right there.

So who the heck was Lorraine Sandoval?

It wasn't until I was halfway back to The Haven that I remembered the Mexican guy who crashed his car getting mangoes for Mallory. Pablo, the assistant director. The night I ran into Kendra and Harvy at the Pizza parlor, Kendra said Pablo had been injured badly, that he'd wound up in a wheelchair.

Suddenly a scenario began to take shape in my mind.

What if Cathy/Lorraine was a relative of Pablo's? After all, Sandoval was a Hispanic name. True, Cathy didn't look Hispanic. But what if she was his wife? A wife who'd watched her husband lose the use of his limbs all because of Mallory's idiotic obsession with mangoes.

For years she'd seethed with resentment, until one day she decided to take action. She showed up at The Haven, pretending to be a daffy supermarket checker, all the while plotting to murder the woman who'd ruined her husband's life.

Could it be? Was it possible that all Sven and Shawna were guilty of was theft? And that the woman I knew as Chatty Cathy was the real killer?

Chapter 25

Olga was in the lobby when I got back, making some notes at the reception desk.

For once I was glad to see her. I needed to speak with Kendra, and I had no idea which room she was in.

"Hey, Olga."

She looked up at me and sniffed suspiciously.

"I smell food," she said, staring at the bulges in my sweats.

Out of habit, I'd stashed my goodies in my pockets.

She got up and walked over to me, clad in a somewhat ratty chenille bathrobe, her silver-laced braid dangling down her back.

Ordinarily I would have been trembling in fear before the Diet Nazi. But not now. I had a killer to catch, and I didn't have time for her nonsense.

"Pastrami!" she exclaimed, with a triumphant sniff. "It's pastrami, isn't it?"

"Good for you," I said. "Pastrami and swiss on rye. With a Dove Bar for dessert. Now that we've got that cleared up, tell me: Where's Kendra's room?"

She gasped at my impudence.

"Just because it's your last night here," she snapped, "doesn't mean you can cheat. Hand it over."

She held out her open palm.

"I will not hand it over!" I snapped right back. "You want a pastrami sandwich, you'll have to drive over to Darryl's and get your own."

Her mouth formed a tiny Cheerio of surprise.

"Now where the hell," I said, grabbing her by her chenille lapels, "is Kendra's room?"

"Upstairs," she said meekly. "Number seven."

Wow, if I'd known it would be this easy standing up to her, I would've tried it ages ago.

"Here," I said, tossing her my Dove Bar as I raced up the stairs. "Don't eat it all in one bite."

Seconds later, I was banging on Kendra's door.

I waited impatiently in the hallway until she finally answered it—clad in sexy baby dolls, her hair tousled, the room behind her shrouded in darkness.

"Sorry if I woke you," I said.

"What do you want?" she asked, with more than an edge of irritation in her voice.

"Remember that assistant director in Mexico,

the one Mallory sent to get mangoes in a hurricane?

"Pablo, yes."

"Do you remember his last name?"

She scratched her head. "Gee, I don't know. Sanchez? Fernandez? Jimenez?"

A fat lot of help she was.

"I know his last name."

A shadowy figure got up from the bed and walked over to us. Or I should say swaggered over. It was none other than macho action hero, Clint Masters, who'd apparently been making a special guest appearance on Kendra's mattress. There he was, naked as the day he was born. Except for the marabou-trimmed robe he was holding up in front of his privates.

Whether it was his or Kendra's, I had no idea.

"Sure, I remember Pablo's last name," he said. "It was Sandoval. Pablo Sandoval."

Bingo.

I left Kendra's room, convinced that Chatty Cathy aka Lorraine Sandoval was the killer. It all made perfect sense.

I had to call Brangelina right away and tell them the news.

But I never did get around to it. Because when I got back to my room, I was in for a most unpleasant surprise.

Prozac was missing.

"Prozac, honey," I called out. "Look what Mommy's got you. Yummy smoked salmon!"

But there was no patter of little paws skittering to my side.

And right away I knew something was wrong.

That cat can smell food in Des Moines. She should have been howling at my ankles doing her Feed Me dance.

I hurried to the patio, hoping she might be having a close encounter with her litter box, but no such luck. Then, remembering last night's koi caper, I checked the patio screen. Kevin had stopped by to fix the gap in the mesh earlier that afternoon. But now I saw it had come loose again.

Damn that Kevin. The kid gave new meaning to the word incompetent.

Figuring Prozac had clawed her way out, I headed straight to where I knew I'd find her: The koi pond.

But much to my disappointment, she was nowhere in sight.

By now I was beginning to panic. The Haven was surrounded by woods. What if coyotes were lurking nearby, just waiting to pounce on my precious kitty?

Frantically I started searching the grounds. I checked the garbage pail outside the kitchen (hoping I'd find her swan diving for scraps), the pool area (terrified I'd find her floating in the water), and the organic garden (I knew I'd never find her there).

Then, just as I was passing by the gym, I heard the blessed sound of meowing inside.

Flinging the door open, I breathed a sigh of

relief to see Prozac sitting in a shaft of moonlight.

Thank God there wasn't a koi hanging from
her mouth.

I hurried toward her—wondering for the first
time how she'd been able to open the door—
when suddenly a walloping shove in my back
sent me sprawling to the floor.

Behind me, I heard the door slam shut and
the overhead fluorescent lights click on. When I
looked up, I saw Cathy standing over me, wielding one of The Haven's heavy metal exercise
bars.

Gone was the silly dingbat who'd been plagu-
ing me with her chatter. In her place was a
steely-eyed gal with alarmingly beefy muscles.

"Game's over, Jaine," she said, slapping the
exercise bar into her open palm. "I saw you pick
up my sales receipt."

For a minute I considered playing innocent,
pretending I had no idea what she was talking
about, but I could tell from the steel in her eyes
I'd be wasting my time.

"Now we can do this the hard way," she said,
"where I bash in your skull right now."

I cringed as she swung the exercise bar just
inches from my head.

"Or we can go the easy way, where you do
what I say and there's no bloodshed."

"Plan B," I said. "I vote for Plan B."

"Wise choice. Now get up and start walking.
Over there."

She pointed to the Fat Vat.

You remember the Fat Vat, don't you, that detested egg-shaped contraption Olga used to measure my flab? Now it hovered ominously in the far corner of the room.

What on earth was Cathy/Lorraine up to? Whatever it was, I doubted she'd be doing any measuring.

Prozac, sensing I was in extreme danger, sprang into action and hid behind a treadmill.

I thought of making a run for it, too, but I couldn't risk it. Not with that exercise bar just inches from my cranium. I had to keep Cathy/Lorraine talking and pray someone noticed the light from under the gym door.

"So you're Pablo Sandoval's wife," I said, as I struggled up from the floor.

"Pablo was my hubby, all right. Met him down in Acapulco on vacation. Fell head over heels in love. But then that bitch Mallory came along and ruined everything. Her and her goddamn mangoes."

I tutted in sympathy, hoping to worm my way into her good graces.

"Pablo wound up in a wheelchair, and I spent the next fifteen years taking care of him. He finally died last spring. Shot himself in the mouth." She barked out a bitter laugh. "It's a wonderful life, huh?"

"How awful for you!"

Maybe if I convinced her I was on her side, she'd let me go. I just had to keep nodding and tsking and being her friend.

"Thank God Pablo took out a life insurance policy. It gave me the money I needed to even the score with Mallory. When the little publicity whore tweeted she was going to be staying at The Haven, I decided to book a trip of my own. It was high time she paid for her sins."

"Absolutely!" I commiserated. "Justice served and all that. There's not a jury in the land that would convict you!"

"But I couldn't check in as Lorraine Sandoval. I'd be the first one the cops suspected when Mallory was bumped off. I needed another identity. So my cousin Cathy loaned me her driver's license and credit cards."

"How nice of her," I chimed in, still playing her BFF.

"Well, she didn't exactly loan them to me. Not willingly. Actually she put up a bit of a struggle. Which is why I had to kill her."

"You killed your own cousin?"

"Oh, we weren't very close," she replied breezily. "But luckily we share a family resemblance. It really helped with the photo ID."

Holy Moses! This woman had now entered the serial killer zone.

"Fortunately Cathy had few friends to speak of. And she was on vacation from her job at the Piggly Wiggly. So nobody even knows she's missing."

She shot me a sly smile.

"Except you, of course."

Gulp.

"You know, I warned you to mind your own business."

"So it was you who tried to drown me that day at the jacuzzi."

"Of course it was me. You were snooping

around too damn much. Why do you think I kept hanging around, helping you 'solve' the crime? I wanted to keep an eye on you."

I kicked myself for never suspecting her.

"Too bad we had to bump into each other at the market tonight. My cousin had maxed out her credit cards, so I was reduced to using my own. If only I hadn't dropped my receipt. Rotten luck, wasn't it, hon?"

I didn't like the look in her eyes. A lot like Prozac's when she's about to pounce on my pantyhose.

"I figured you'd figure out the truth, so when I got back to The Haven, I cut open your patio screen and your darling kitty was only too happy to jump into my arms and act as bait to my little trap."

By now we'd reached the Fat Vat.

"I can't very well let you go running to the cops, can I?" Cathy/Lorraine asked with a deadly smile.

"Oh, but I won't! It'll be our little secret. Honest. Cross my heart."

Somehow I failed to convince her.

"In you go!" And without any further ado, she opened the door to the Fat Vat and shoved me inside.

So much for BFFs.

Then she slammed the door shut and jammed her exercise bar under the levered handle.

"There." She smiled, satisfied. "Tight as a drum."

Her voice was faint through the thick walls of the vat.

Oh, God. This thing was like a coffin. I sat on its tiny metal bench, peering out from the reinforced glass window, with barely any room to move. With each breath I took, I could feel myself sucking up the air inside.

"With any luck," Cathy/Lorraine said, "you'll run out of oxygen in an hour or so. And if not, it won't matter. I'll be on a plane to a faraway country that doesn't believe in extradition.

"Ta ta," she said with a jaunty wave, and started for the door.

She couldn't just leave me to die like this. I'd rather have been conked over the head with the exercise bar.

I started screaming at the top of my lungs.

"Don't waste your breath, hon," she called back over her shoulder. "Nobody will be able hear you. Not from inside that thing."

And then, with a final wave, she was gone.

Panic rising, I tried to open the Fat Vat's door from the inside, working the handle as hard as I could, but it was jammed tight thanks to that damn exercise bar. I tried smashing the window with my running shoe, but the glass was like steel.

Finally, hoping against hope someone would hear me, I pounded on the window, screaming for help. But it was no use.

I cursed myself for all the oxygen I'd wasted. Who knew how long I had left before I sucked it all up?

Oh, God! I didn't want to die. Not here. Not now. Not in a stupid Fat Vat!

My only solace was the thought of Lance

bawling his eyes out at my funeral, blaming himself for my untimely death.

Yeah, right. If I knew Lance, he'd shed a few tears and then start making a play for one of the pallbearers.

I was sitting there, promising God I would give up Chunky Monkey forever if only She'd get me out of this mess, when Prozac came trotting out from behind the treadmill.

Dear, sweet, Prozac. I was going to miss her so! Her funny little Feed Me dance, her quaint habit of clawing my cashmere sweaters to ribbons, her pooping in my boots when she was pissed at me—

Okay, so we had our issues, but doesn't every couple?

Now she looked up at me with big green eyes that seemed to say:

Where the heck is my snack???

And then it hit me.

Prozac's snack! It could be my ticket to salvation!

Rummaging around in my pockets, I found the smoked salmon I'd bought for her at Darryl's what seemed like centuries ago. I ripped open the plastic with my teeth, then held up a strip of the bright orange delicacy in the Fat Vat window.

"Look!" I shouted. "Yummy smoked salmon!"

Prozac's eyes lit up with lust, and she began clawing at the door of the Fat Vat, somehow hoping to get it open.

A waste of time, of course.

This trick may have served her well with the kitchen cupboards at home, but it'd never work on the Fat Vat. The only way she'd be able to open the door was to dislodge that damn exercise bar.

I banged on the glass window to get her attention, then waved the piece of salmon at eye level with the exercise bar.

Now she got the idea. With an impressive leap, she landed on the exercise bar, hoping to get at the salmon. Unfortunately the bar didn't budge, and don't think she wasn't mighty peeved. Even through the Fat Vat's thick window I could hear her high decibel yowls of disappointment.

But Prozac is nothing if not persistent.

She tried again. And again. And again. After her fourth attempt, I thought I saw the exercise bar move.

"Keep going, honey!" I shouted. "You're almost there!"

And then, with one last flying leap, all those years of overeating finally paid off. The exercise bar gave way to her weight and came clattering to the ground.

Thanks to my clever feline snackaholic, I was free!

With trembling hands I let myself out of the Fat Vat, and scooped her up in my arms.

"Oh, Prozac, sweetheart, how can I ever thank you?"

You can start with that salmon.

"Of course," I said, quickly tearing her treat into bite sized morsels.

She dug in with gusto, then gazed up at me in that cute little way she has, as if to say:

What? No crème fraiche?

This touching little reunion was interrupted when Olga came storming in to the gym in her chenille bathrobe, braid flying.

"What on earth is going on? I heard your cat yowling all the way from my room."

I gave her a brief recap of recent events and she quickly put in a call to Brangelina, who managed to apprehend Cathy/Lorraine just as she was about to board a connecting flight for Mozambique.

Meanwhile Prozac and I were nestled in Olga's kitchen, celebrating my escape from the Fat Vat with pastrami and smoked salmon. Plus a bonus slab of cheesecake.

By now the other guests had woken up and wandered in to join us, eager to know what the fuss was all about.

Unfortunately my mouth was filled with pastrami at the time, so Olga told them about my confrontation with Cathy. When she was finished, they gazed in my direction with newfound respect.

"Why that's the bravest thing I've ever heard!" Kendra said.

"Amazing!" Clint agreed, flashing his pearlies in approval.

"What a heroine!" Harvy gushed.

I smiled modestly.

"Can I pet her?"

Huh???

"Can I pet your cat? I can't get over the way the little darling came to your rescue and saved your life."

Prozac preened.

I don't know what she'd do without me.

Oh, for crying out loud. What about me? Jaine Austen? The gal who risked her life bringing Mallory's killer to justice?

"She's such a pretty little thing," Clint said, stroking her behind the ears. "And so well behaved. She ought to be in movies."

Prozac looked up at him with worshipful eyes and purred.

I'm ready for my close up, Mr. Masters.

Oh, for crying out loud. What a ham. Any minute now, she'd be doing the balcony scene from *Romeo & Juliet*.

"Why can't you be more like Prozac?" Kendra chided Armani, who was watching the proceedings from the crook of her arm.

To which Armani let out a vicious growl.

I knew just how he felt.

Bright and early the next morning, I checked out of The Haven, and in a touching gesture of gratitude, Delphine offered to carry my luggage to the parking lot for only five bucks.

It was with happy heart indeed that I got in my Corolla and drove off from Diet Hell, two and a half pounds heavier than when I checked in.

YOU'VE GOT MAIL

Tampa Vistas Tattler
Candidate Charged with Indecent Exposure

A citation has been issued to Tampa Vistas resident Hank Austen for showing up at the recent presidential debate in I ♥ My Gnome boxer shorts. "His behavior was totally inappropriate," claimed Lydia Pinkus, who won the election in an unprecedented 798-to-1 landslide, "and an insult to our viewers."

"With legs like his," added Channel 99 producer Artie Myers, "the guy should stick to long johns."

Austen has been banned from the clubhouse for three months, and from the Channel 99 studio forever.

To: Jausten
From: DaddyO
Subject: Little Snafu

Dearest Lambchop—

I suppose by now you've heard about the little snafu at the debate. I'm afraid your mom was a bit miffed, but I managed to worm my way back into her good graces with a dozen roses and some chocolates.

And I'm sorry to say I lost the election by a rather wide margin. Unbelievable, isn't it? If you ask me, Lydia rigged the votes. But Mom threatened to divorce me if I demanded a recount, so I guess for the time being, I'll have to retire from politics.

Try not to be too upset, sweetheart. I may have lost the vote, but I won a moral victory. I can hold my head high, knowing I went to bat for my poor, downtrodden gnomes.

By the way, I'm sending you one for your apartment. I know you're going to love him. His name is Morty.

Love 'n hugs,

Daddy

To: Jausten
From: Shoptillyoudrop
Subject: Seven Hundred Ninety-Eight to One!

As you can see from the *Tattler*, Daddy lost the election, 798 to 1. And you'll never guess who the one person was who voted for him—Lydia Pinkus!! That's right. Daddy wasn't allowed to vote (he's been banned from the clubhouse) and I was too upset to even bother.

Dear, sweet Lydia, figuring Daddy wasn't going to get any votes, took pity on him. Isn't she just the most wonderful person? And now Daddy is accusing her of rigging the votes! I tell you, honey, that man is impossible. I'd be absolutely furious with him if it weren't for the chocolates he gave me. Nougats with cashews. My favorite. It's hard to stay angry with chocolate in your mouth.

And best news of all—Daddy's finally going to take those god-awful gnomes off the lawn. Hallelujah!

Well, I'm off to my Aztec & Incan history class!

Con mucho amor,

Mom

To: Jausten
From: DaddyO
Subject: Great News!

Great news, Lambchop!

I took the gnomes off the lawn and found an even better place for them—the living room!

They sure brighten up this dull old space.

Can't wait to show 'em to your mom!

Love,

Daddy

Epilogue

Mallory Francis fans everywhere will be happy to know that Cathy (aka Lorraine Sandoval) is in jail awaiting trial for murder.

In related news, several crew members who'd worked with Mallory have banded together to start the Lorraine Sandoval Defense Fund. So far, contributions have totaled more than $972,000.

Kendra decided not to press charges against Sven and Shawna for stealing Mallory's necklace, and last I heard, the Aerobics Twins were working at a Bally's in West Covina.

As for Kendra, it turns out she and Armani are getting along just fine. More than fine, now that Armani's bringing home the big bucks. That's right. Kendra took Armani to doggie obedience school, where he was discovered by a Hollywood talent scout. One thing led to another and the little pooch is now starring as

"Butch, the Killer Peke" in *Revenge of the Lust Busters, Part II.*

Kendra is acting as his personal trainer. Rumor has it she's dating Clint Masters.

More good news: Harvy's salon has been discovered by the Beverly Hills fashionista set and is doing wonderfully well.

Rumor has it he's dating Clint Masters, too.

Business at The Haven has been booming ever since Olga took on Delphine as her business partner. (Trust me, some day that kid will be running IBM.) Grateful for my work in cracking the case, Olga sent me a ginormous gluten-free, low-calorie muffin gift basket. (It comes in quite handy as a doorstop.)

And finally, in the Dreams Really Do Come True Department, Kevin the cook is now a busboy at Applebee's.

As for Lance, it took me a while, but I finally forgave him. Last week he took me out for a chateaubriand dinner-for-two with all the trimmings. (Lance had the poached fish.)

Prozac is happy as a clam to be back home with snacks on tap 24/7. Although sometimes in her more pensive moments, she gets this faraway look in her eyes, and I know she's thinking of The Koi that Got Away.

Well, gotta run and feed Her Highness before my date shows up. That's right. I, Jaine Austen, charter member of the Saturday Night Pizza-for-One Club, have actually got a date.

In the Dreams Really Do Come True Department, Part II, Darryl is coming to town to see me. I've invited him to my apartment for a home-cooked Italian dinner—Caesar salad, lasagna, and tiramisu for dessert.

It should be ready any minute now, just as soon as the delivery guy shows up.

Please turn the page for an exciting sneak peek
of Laura Livine's next Jaine Austen mystery
DEATH OF A NEIGHBORHOOD WITCH
coming in September 2012!

Chapter 1

I dashed into the market for a carton of orange juice. I swear, that's all. An innocent carton of orange juice.

But then I saw it. The giant display of Halloween candies, luring me with their shiny wrappers, a siren song of chocolate in a sea of nuts and caramel.

I tried to pretend they weren't there, but it was no use. I could practically hear the Mini Snickers calling my name:

Jaine, sweetheart! We're only seventy-two luscious calories. Surely just one can't hurt, can it?

Like the chocolate junkie I am, I fell for their come-on. Before I knew it, I was loading my cart with those sneaky Snickers, along with some Kit Kats and Reese's Pieces.

It's the same old story, I'm afraid. Every year I vow not to buy any Halloween candy. And every year, like the sniveling weakling I am, I break that vow.

The truth is I have absolutely no need for Halloween candy. Here in the slums of Beverly Hills where I live, south of Wilshire Boulevard (so south it's practically in Mexico), there are very few children. People on my block are either singletons or retirees. The only trick-or-treaters who've ever shown up on my doorstep were a pair of surly teens with squinty eyes and multiple body piercings. And I'm guessing all they wound up with at the end of the night was a bagful of restraining orders.

By now I was at the checkout counter, my orange juice long forgotten.

"Just stocking up for the trick-or-treaters," I lied to the checker, a hardened blonde with thin lips and a concrete beehive. "Can't disappoint the kiddies."

The checker snapped her gum, oozing skepticism. She knew darn well the only one who'd be chomping down on those candies was me.

At the last minute, I threw in a miniature pumpkin, painted with a happy face, hoping to convince her of my Halloween spirit, but she still wasn't buying my "for the kiddies" act.

I heard her whisper to the bag boy as I walked away, "Ten to one she'll be breaking into those Snickers at the first stoplight."

How utterly ridiculous.

I didn't break into them until the third stoplight.

Back home, I found my cat, Prozac, doing

battle with a pair of my brand-new panty hose. How she manages to raid my underwear drawer I'll never know. But there she was, tearing into my Control Top Donna Karans with all the gusto of a Jersey Housewife on estrogen.

"Prozac! What are you doing?!"

She shot me an impatient stare.

Vanquishing the enemy, of course!

Then back to my Donna Karans.

Die, spandex infidel! Die!

After wrestling what was left of my panty hose from her claws, I started unloading my groceries. When I took out the miniature painted pumpkin and put it on the counter, Prozac's eyes widened in alarm.

Omigod! An evil vegetable from the Planet Carotene!

One look at the goofy painted face with the crossed eyes and missing front teeth, and she forgot all about her war with my panty hose. Before I could stop her, she leaped onto the counter, digging her claws into Pumpkin Face.

"Cut that out," I said, whipping it away from her. "This is a perfectly harmless pumpkin, and I'll thank you to keep your paws to yourself."

With that, I trotted over to the door and put the pumpkin outside on my front step.

"You'll be safe here," I said, giving it a little pat.

Not really.

Like a furry missile, Prozac whizzed out from behind me and, snapping up the pumpkin's stem in her jaws, took off like a shot. I chased her up the street and groaned to see her bounding up the path to a once elegant but now dilapidated old house.

Of all the houses on the block, why did she have to choose this one?

The crumbling Spanish hacienda belonged to the neighborhood witch, a grouch royale named Cryptessa Muldoon. That wasn't her real name, of course. That was the name of the character she played, decades ago, on a third-rate sitcom—a sorry cross between *Bewitched* and *The Munsters*—called *I Married a Zombie*. Cryptessa was the zombie in question, delivering her lines in a long black wig and slinky dress cut so tight it was practically a tourniquet. After one laugh-free season, the show had been canceled, and Cryptessa, as everyone on the block still called her, never worked again. Which over time had turned her into a bitter, whackadoodle dame.

She'd been living on the block ever since I could remember, growling at me whenever I'd had the temerity to park my car in front of her house.

I'd tried my best to stay under her radar, and up until that moment, I'd pretty much succeeded.

But all that was about to change.

Now as I raced past her DO NOT TRESPASS sign, desperately trying to catch up with Prozac, Cryptessa came bursting out of her front door, eyeing me with wild-eyed paranoia. No longer the least bit slinky, she wore ketchup-stained sweats, her stringy hair dyed a most startling shade of shoe-polish black.

"Hi there!" I said, hoping to disarm her with a friendly wave.

Alas, it did not work.

"Get off my property," she shrieked, "or I'll call the police!"

"Absolutely," I assured her, "just as soon as I get Prozac."

"What do you think I am, a pharmacist? I don't have any Prozac."

"No, my cat, Prozac."

I dashed around the side of the house, where I found Prozac staring transfixed into Cryptessa's window, Pumpkin Face lying abandoned in the grass.

Following her gaze into the open window, I saw a dull green parakeet perched on wobbly legs in a cage, feathers mottled with age.

The poor thing had been minding his own business, no doubt dreaming fond dreams of juicy worms, when he looked down and saw Prozac staring up at him. I guess he must have seen the bloodlust in her eyes. Because without any further ado, he let out a strangled peep and proceeded to keel over.

"Omigod!" cried Cryptessa, who'd raced up to the window. "You've killed Van Helsing! You've killed Van Helsing!"

And indeed, the poor little critter had kicked the bucket.

"I'm so very sorry," I said. "But really, I didn't do a thing. I was just standing here."

"You've killed Van Helsing!" Cryptessa wailed again, unable to let go of the thought.

"I know it's small consolation for the loss of

your beloved pet, but I hope you'll accept this colorful Halloween pumpkin as a token of my apology."

I held out Pumpkin Face.

"Get the hell out of here!" she shrieked.

Only too happy to oblige, I grabbed Prozac and scooted off to freedom, leaving the pumpkin behind, just in case Cryptessa changed her mind.

Back home, I read Prozac the riot act.

"Bad kitty! Very bad kitty! You ran away from home and scared a poor little parakeet to death! Whatever am I going to do with you?"

She looked up at me from where I'd plopped her on the sofa.

I'd suggest a nice long belly rub, with some bonus scratching behind my ears.

I'm ashamed to confess that, after a calming Mini Snickers or three, I was actually in the middle of giving her that belly rub when I heard a loud banging at my front door.

I opened it to find Cryptessa standing there, eyes blazing, her shoe-polish hair standing out in angry spikes.

"You killed him. Now you have to help me bury him."

"Pardon me?"

"I need you to dig a hole for Van Helsing's grave. I can't do it. Not with my bad back."

"Of course, of course. I'd be more than happy to."

I wouldn't have been so damn happy if I'd known what was in store for me.

* * *

I followed Cryptessa to her backyard, a land-scaping nightmare with ancient patio furniture, spider-infested bushes, and a ragged patch of dying weeds posing as a lawn.

"Watch out for the oil slicks," she warned, too late, as I stepped in a puddle of black goo. "Gardener's damn lawnmower keeps leaking."

I looked down in dismay at the new pair of Reeboks I'd just taken out of the box that morning. They'd never be white again.

Cryptessa had chosen a shady spot under a hulking magnolia tree for Van Helsing's final resting place.

"Start digging," she said, handing me a rusty shovel.

The soil, clearly not having been watered in the last two decades, was like cement, and before long I was gushing sweat. Not happy with a shallow grave, Cryptessa made me dig at least three feet below the surface. When at last the grave had been dug to her satisfaction, she barked, "Wait here!"

And then she disappeared into the house.

I stood leaning on my shovel for a good fifteen minutes before she finally came sailing back out again in a long, black, moth-eaten dress, with matching veil—stolen no doubt from the wardrobe department of *I Married a Zombie*. In her hand she carried the "coffin"—a Payless shoe box, lined in pink Kleenex, Van Helsing's stiff little body nestled in the folds.

Then, gazing into his beady eye with all the

pathos of a failed sitcom actress, she began
singing:

The way you held your beak
The way you sang off key
The way you used to shriek
No, no, they can't take that away from me

The way your wings just flopped
The way you chirped "twee twee"
The way your poops just popped
No, no, they can't take that away from me

Wiping a tear from her eye, she put the lid on
Van Helsing's coffin and slowly lowered him
into the grave. I had no doubt that somewhere
out there the Gershwin brothers were rolling
over in theirs. Then, as Cryptessa hummed "Taps,"
I filled in the earth.

At last, my ordeal was over. Or so I thought.

"As long as you're here," Cryptessa said,
"would you mind planting these for me?"

She pointed to a bed of bright pink petunias
by her fence.

"I'd do it myself," she said with a long-suffering
smile, "but my back is killing me."

So is mine, lady, was what I felt like saying.

But, still feeling guilty about Van Helsing, I
picked up the shovel and started digging.

I spent the next half hour on my hands and
knees, jamming petunias and potting mix into
the concrete soil. Cryptessa stood over me, much
as I imagine Simon Legree must have done down

on the plantation, barking orders and hollering at me not to bruise the leaves.

Finally, when every petunia had been planted, she released me from captivity. My fingernails cracked and filled with dirt, my Reeboks stained black, I trudged back to my apartment, cursing Cryptessa every step of the way.

My mood took a slight turn for the cheerier, however, when I got to my duplex and found an absolute cutie pie of a guy ringing my doorbell.

"Oh, hello," he said when he saw me coming up the path. "I'm Peter Connor. I just moved in up the street and dropped by to say hi."

"Nice to meet you," I said.

Indeed it was. There was something about this guy's smile that radiated kindness. And I badly needed a dose of the stuff. I was still licking my wounds from yet another failed relationship with a guy named Darryl who I'd met up in central California. He'd been driving down to see me on weekends, bunking with an old college buddy of his. Before long, love blossomed, and Darryl proposed marriage. Not to me, I'm afraid. But to his old college buddy, a pert redhead named Tatiana.

So when I saw Peter standing there that day, smiling that sweet smile and looking like the kind of guy who would never fall in love with his old college buddy, my heart melted just a tad.

Now he held out his hand to shake mine, and I suddenly remembered my filthy fingernails. And sweaty armpits. And heaven only knew what my hair must have looked like. I'm guessing Early Bride of Frankenstein.

"You'll have to excuse me," I said. "I've just been gardening and I'm afraid I'm a mess."

"You look fine to me."

And I have to say, the feeling was mutual.

As noted before, Peter was one primo cutie pie: slim yet muscular, with a shock of thick sandy hair, soft brown eyes, and—just beneath that sweet smile—the most amazing cleft in his chin.

I happen to find chin clefts immensely attractive. It was all I could do not to run my finger along his. But of course I didn't. I knew the rules. I knew how to play it cool.

"Anyhow," he said, shooting me a winning grin, "I'm throwing a little housewarming party, and I was hoping you could stop by."

"I'd love it. Absolutely. I'll be there! For sure!"

So much for playing it cool.

"Sunday at about three o'clock?"

"Can't wait!" I gushed.

"See you then," he said, heading down the path.

I sailed into my apartment on cloud nine. True, the whole Van Helsing funeral thing had been a bit of a downer. But on the upside, it looked like I had just met a potential soul mate.

Ah, yes, I thought as I trotted off to the shower. Things were definitely looking up.

How wrong I was.

Dead wrong.